Lenny stepped past Karnowsk behind the tall man. One of woman who hired him. To one s. thick glasses, while on her other side Lenny's gaze was drawn to a striking young woman, not just for her artfully applied makeup and her long red hair, but her totally tight, totally black costume—suit, blouse, stockings and sensible heels. She looked like she was dressed in business gothic.

"These are all members of your team," Ms. Siggenbottom began brusquely.

Team? Lenny almost said out loud.

"Karnowski he has met!" the tall man said with a deep breath of pride. "But her does not know my title. I am Karnoswki the Ghost Finder!"

Ghost finder? Lenny swallowed those words as well.

Lenny thought he should say something. "And I'll be working with all of you?"

"All of *them*," Ms. Siggenbottom agreed. "And one more. There is a team member we can only meet after dark."

The others nodded as if this was only to be understood.

"But I have neglected to introduce our final member," the older woman continued. "The young woman is named Lenore."

The young woman stepped forward, her well penciled brow creasing with effort. Lenny found her strangely attractive—where his old girlfriend was bright and bubbly, this Lenore had an air of the mysterious about her.

Her voice was a low whisper. "Say nothing."

Copyright © 2016 by Craig Shaw Gardner
Cover by Cortney Skinner
Design by Aaron Rosenberg
ISBN 978-1-941408-91-9 — ISBN 978-1-941408-92-6 (pbk)
All rights reserved. No part of this book may be used or reproduced in any manner whatsoever without written permission except in the case of brief quotations embodied in critical articles and reviews.
For information address Crossroad Press at 141 Brayden Dr., Hertford, NC 27944
www.crossroadpress.com

First edition

Temporary Monsters

CRAIG SHAW GARDNER

One

Maybe this time would be different.

Lenny Hodge took a deep breath. He had to keep a positive attitude. He stood in the hallway, staring at the gold letters (outlined in black) painted on the frosted glass.

TERRIFITEMPS!
WE'VE GOT THE ANSWERS!

The door, the hallway with its greenish-gray linoleum floor and glass light fixtures, even the old wrought-iron elevator that had brought him up here, all of it seemed from another time and place. All the other temp agencies in greater Boston—and he had seen close to a dozen—were in brand-new buildings, all state-of-the-art chrome and glass and modern art prints and attractive greenery; places that said "We're the cutting edge"; places where he could fill out endless forms. So they could never call him back...

This place said something more like "Welcome to 1962!" Not that it mattered. Lenny had passed desperate a long time ago. Nobody was hiring. He still went out on every interview he could find—more from habit than anything else. Maybe an old-fashioned place would give him brand-new results.

He took another deep breath and opened the door.

Lenny stepped into a large reception room, as dimly lit and colorless as the corridor outside. The same greenish-gray tile stretched across the floor, no sign of carpeting anywhere. Gray molded chairs lined the walls and formed an island in the room's center. Despite the many chairs, almost every seat was filled. At the far end of the room was a large metal desk. An older woman in a gray business suit sat behind it. Her gray hair was pulled back into a severe bun. He couldn't imagine her having any expression other than her current frown as she shuffled papers from one pile to another. She certainly seemed too busy to acknowledge Lenny or the dozens of others in the room before her.

That was it; chairs, linoleum, harsh fluorescent light. Not a potted plant in sight. Some of those who were seated scowled at him over ancient magazines. The older woman barely looked up as he approached the desk.

"Over there," she announced with a jerk of her head before Lenny could say a word. He turned and found an empty seat in the sea of chairs.

Those around him barely glanced up as he sat in their midst. He guessed now that, since the woman had acknowledged him, he was one of the crowd. Lenny also guessed he was in for a very long wait. From the glazed expressions on the others' faces, they could have been sitting here since the day this place had opened.

His chair sat next to a small Formica table piled high with magazines. He glanced through them quickly. Colliers? Argosy? Divination Quarterly? The whole pile was the same. He hadn't heard of most of these titles. He could swear that some of the others hadn't been published in years.

Lenny realized he couldn't let any of this distract him. This agency needed the right kind of answers and Lenny was going to be ready. He had to give them positive, motivated responses, as if he actually knew what he wanted to do with his life.

Lenny sighed. He was sure he had a lot of talent, if he was only given a chance to find it. Well, his résumé could be a little stronger. In the last three years, he had had four jobs, none lasting over six months. Bad luck mostly. Like the massive sewage backup with the giant alligators that time he was working security. How could anyone blame that on him? And it certainly wasn't his fault when the Russian spy satellite came crashing out of the sky, demolishing the Dairy Freeze five minutes before he was scheduled to open. And then there was the escape of the superintelligent gerbils, just when he was cleaning up the lab. How had he known that when he accidentally switched the feed—well, he didn't have to talk about that one, did he?

"Mr. Hodge?"

Lenny looked up. He had barely had a chance to sit and get anxious. He stood and pointed at his chest.

"Yes, Mr. Hodge." The woman at the desk nodded in his direction. "Ms. Siggenbottom will see you now."

Lenny stood, so astonished he hardly noticed the angry stares of all those seated around him. He hadn't filled out a form, he hadn't spoken, and he certainly hadn't mentioned his name to anyone.

A job was a job was a job, he reminded himself. Stay positive, no matter what.

The woman nodded at a door to her right.

He walked across the worn linoleum to the door, doing his best to breathe, and read the gold lettering (outlined in black) on the frosted glass as he approached:

HELENE WAXWORTH SIGGENBOTTOM
DIRECTOR OF PERSONNEL

Stay positive. Concentrate on what was important. He was going to get an interview.

He knocked. A woman's deep voice told him to come in.

He opened the door, and saw a room that looked a lot like the waiting room, same gray metal desk, same gray plastic chairs. His attention was immediately drawn to the woman behind the desk.

She was almost the twin of the woman out front. Her hair was perhaps a little whiter, her severe business suit a little darker. And her stare was even more intimidating.

"About time," she barked as she glared at him. "We were beginning to think you'd never get here."

"Pardon?" Lenny felt like he had stepped into the middle of someone else's conversation.

She waved him to the plastic chair nearest the desk.

"Have a seat, Mr. Hodge. Before we go any further, I have a few important questions."

"Yes ma'am." She was a ma'am if he had ever seen one. Lenny sat.

She glanced for an instant at the papers before her, then resumed her disapproving stare.

"Do you have any problem working with people who are different?"

What did that mean? Lenny searched for an answer.

"Aren't we all different?"

She grunted and wrote something down on the paper.

"Now," she announced, staring even more intently at Lenny than before.

Loud noises came from somewhere nearby, maybe the room on the other side of her office, just beyond another door of frosted glass. The sounds were high and quick. They might have been screams. They might have been laughter. Whatever they were, Lenny decided they were very odd.

Ms. Siggenbottom glanced at the far door. "That's nothing to be concerned about. Are you concerned?"

"Should I be?"

She nodded as if that was exactly the answer she was looking for. "Duly noted." She pressed a button on her desk. The noises stopped.

She looked down at her papers and began to read "A hippogriff boards a train in London, that proceeds north at forty kilometers per hour. Fifteen minutes later, a traditional witch starts flying from Glasgow, going south five kilometers faster than the train. Midway between the two, the stationmaster is eating a sandwich. . . ."

Lenny was having trouble paying attention. Where were the questions about his work goals and aspirations—his strengths and weaknesses? It was like he had been rehearsing for Macbeth and then realized he was in the middle of Waiting for Godot.

"—and the wind is blowing at seven knots from the west," Ms. Siggenbottom droned on. Lenny realized he had missed something. "Now, Mr. Hodge, what color was the stationmaster's cap?"

"Uh—blue?" It was the first thing that had popped into his head.

"Blue. Very interesting." She turned to her papers and wrote at some length, only looking up when a loud pounding began to Lenny's left. Lenny glanced over to see something large and black pounding on the window, a hulking shape with glowing eyes. No, not eyes. What Lenny had taken for the thing's face actually swirled with iridescent color, until it formed a single word: beware.

"Interesting," his interviewer said calmly, as if black shapes bearing glowing messages showed up at her fourteenth-floor window every day.

"What was that?" Lenny asked as he looked back to the Ms. Siggenbottom.

"Sometimes the wind can make funny noises in these old buildings," she replied as she continued to write.

Wind? Lenny looked back at the window, out at the sunny sky. The black shape was gone. How? Why? Lenny was even more confused. Had he imagined everything?

Ms. Siggenbottom put down her pen. "Well, Mr. Hodge. Considering your past experience . . ." She paused and wrote some more. Lenny remembered he still hadn't shown anyone his résumé. "... and your very interesting answers," she continued, "I believe we have only one course of action."

Here it comes, Lenny thought. The same heave-ho he had heard a dozen times before.

Ms. Siggenbottom lifted her head to stare at Lenny once more. Lenny realized there was something different about her, especially her lower face. Her mouth had twisted upward ever so slightly, as though she were attempting to actually smile.

"I have only one more question," she announced. "When can you start?"

Lenny did his best to keep his mouth closed and smile back. They were actually going to hire him? What should he say? It was a Thursday. He didn't want to appear too eager.

"How about Monday?"

"Perfectly reasonable. We have something very special lined up for you, Mr. Hodge. But I believe you'll do splendidly. We'll see you here at nine a.m. on Monday." She glanced at his interview coat and tie. "Oh yes. And a suit is not required."

She pointed toward the office behind her.

"It is better if you go out the back. It is best if you enter that way on Monday as well. The door has a buzzer. Just ring and someone will let you in."

Lenny thanked her and turned to go. He had a job. Who cared what odd little rules went along with it?

He opened the back door and stepped into another room that looked almost exactly like the other offices. Except that the gray metal desk in here was occupied by a tall, pale man dressed in black. The cut of his suit seemed old-fashioned, almost Victorian. Lenny decided that if the man wore a stovepipe hat, he could pass for an undertaker from a hundred years ago.

The man nodded as Lenny closed the door behind him.

"Mr. Hodge?"

So everyone knew his name? Lenny nodded.

"You are one of us, now, eh?" The man's smile made his face look a bit like a skull. "We welcome you to team."

Lenny thanked him as the man returned to looking at the file folder in his hands. "We will see you Monday," he called over his shoulder.

Lenny knew that was his cue to leave. He stepped out into the hallway, maybe fifty feet away from where he had entered. The door swung closed and locked behind him, but not before Lenny heard the man in black say two final words.

"Poor bastard."

Two

Lenny clicked off the alarm as soon as it started to beep. He hadn't really been sleeping. The reality of Monday morning and a brand-new job filled his head. But what kind of a job? And what was with that temp agency?

Lenny sat up and sighed. The initial excitement of someone actually wanting to hire him was long gone. Instead, the weekend had left him with an awful lot of questions.

Not that he hadn't looked for answers. But Terrifitemps didn't even have a website. His next step was to google their name—but even then the citations were rare and sparse. Apparently a few people had found some well-paying short-term employment from the agency, and only regretted there hadn't been more. Most of the comments were complaints about waiting in the Terrifitemps lobbies for hours. (They at least had some other offices, apparently in Cleveland and Boca Raton.) Lenny couldn't find a single blog or bulletin board that mentioned skipping past the wait and getting hired on the spot. Or any further details about someone who actually worked there. In fact, all the entries, both pro and con, lacked detail. Everything about Terrifitemps was sort of vague. As vague as the way the agency had hired him.

People blogged about everything—getting stuck in a line at the registry, breaking up with your boyfriend, eating a ham sandwich—everything but Terrifitemps. Was there some sort of nondisclosure thing at work here? Lenny shook his head. Nondisclosure for a temp agency?

So what had happened to the others like him, who had breezed right through the system? It might be rare, but he couldn't be the only one. Were the others too busy to blog? Or had something else happened to them?

Because that wasn't the weirdest thing about last week's interview. He had never told them anything about himself, hadn't filled in a form, hadn't given them any information at all. Yet Ms. Siggenbottom knew at least his name and maybe even more. It was as if she had been expecting him.

Lenny took a deep breath. This was crazy talk. Terrifitemps had offered him work. He was just having a super case of new-job jitters. Not surprising, since it had been months since he had gotten a paycheck for anything.

This was the part Lenny didn't like to think about. His job history was—a little strange. And his love life? You needed money to have a love life. He thought about Sheila and the last time he had managed to have a steady girlfriend. They had met briefly the summer before, when he had gone back home to visit his mother. They talked about all the fun they'd had together their senior year of high school, and when they had reconnected that summer between semesters of college. At times, he'd thought there might still be something between them—but that was another life, before he had been thrown out into the world, living in a threadbare apartment, unable to hold a job.

He rolled out of bed. Think positive. A job is a job is a job. Maybe they'd actually give him something long-term. Maybe he could meet someone like Sheila and start dating again.

What could happen in an office like that, after all? It was a temp agency, and an out-of-date one at that. What was the worst-case scenario? They offer him a job cleaning elephant cages? It was better than sitting around his apartment with no money. If it was too awful—hey, he could always turn the job down.

Right now he needed coffee—the cheaper stuff he made himself. He rubbed his eyes and pulled on a pair of pants, just in case his roommate had company. He walked into the living room of their shared two-bedroom apartment, decorated, as he liked to call it in "early poverty." Bare wood floor, free posters tacked to the wall, a lumpy thing that might once have been called a sofa under the window.

A job is a job is a job, he thought again. So what if he hadn't worked in months and months? Why was he so worried?

On Friday, he had decided he only had one recourse. He had set up the card table next to the couch, so that he could do the one thing that always helped him when he was stressed—work on his stamp collection. His grandmother had helped him start it when he was eight, and he had kept it with him for close to twenty years, hauling it out whenever he needed to cool down—like the day Sheila had walked out of their relationship, or the eternal waiting to see if he had gotten into his favorite college, or especially after a couple of those bizarre, job-ending accidents that he'd suffered through—who knew those scientists had developed a penguin that could actually fly?

This whole Terrifitemps experience, as happy as he was to get the job, had brought his stress levels up again. So he had brought out his stamp albums one by one and puttered through them for an hour here and there until he was calm enough to do something else. Well, on Saturday, he had needed a couple hours at a time to center himself. Sunday, he worked from about 11:00 a.m. until—oh, about 11:00 p.m. By about 10:30 on Sunday night, he had even looked at the prize of his collection, the Moldavian 3 slotznic first day cover, although he hadn't taken it out of its Mylar sleeve.

But that was all over now. Today he had a job. He'd have to put his stamps away—as soon as he made some coffee.

Somebody rang the doorbell.

At quarter of eight in the morning?

"Bruce?" Lenny called, hoping against hope that his roommate was actually here for a change. As usual, no one answered. Bruce and Denise must be at her place. Bruce and Lenny had met each other in college, been friends ever since, shared their ups and downs—except Bruce seemed to be able to keep his jobs. Not to mention a steady girlfriend. Lenny felt a sudden panic. He hardly saw the two of them anymore. What if Bruce decided to move out?

All the more reason to take this job.

It must be one of the neighbors. Not that Lenny and his roommate knew much of anything about the other people in the building, but— Lenny decided to go see who it was. He stepped up to the door to look through the spyhole, and looked at someone he had never expected to see again.

He slid back the chain and unlocked the two deadbolts as quickly as possible.

"Sheila?" he asked as he opened the door.

His college high school girlfriend smiled back at him from the hall. She looked much the same as the last time he had seen her this past summer. Her long, blonde hair was shorter now, cut just shy of her shoulders, and her cream-colored business suit spoke of a life in business rather than summers down at the beach. But her lightly freckled skin, her eyes that looked blue in some light and green in others, the warmth of her smile— none of those had changed at all.

"Hi!" she said brightly, as if showing up at your ex-boyfriend's door at eight in the morning was the most natural thing possible.

"Uh, hi," Lenny replied. He had trouble coming up with what to say next. After standing there for a moment, he decided to try. "Uh, do you want to come in for a minute?"

She walked past him into the apartment before he had finished the sentence. By the time he closed the door, Sheila was staring down at the card table in the middle of the living room.

"You still collect stamps!" she called over her shoulder. "That's wonderful!"

It was? He seemed to remember, back when they were dating, that Sheila had found the whole stamp thing boring, or annoying, or maybe both.

"Uh, yeah," he replied as he walked over behind her. "Listen, I've got to go out in a few minutes."

She turned and smiled again, looking straight into his eyes. "Here I go and show up without calling. I was in the neighborhood and—impulsive me—I just wanted to see you."

"Uh, well, it's nice to see you, too." Lenny smiled back. How did she know where he lived? Lenny's mother, most likely. She was always trying to get the two of them back together. And right now, Lenny realized, he was glad his mother had interfered.

"I'm glad you think so," Sheila said, stepping closer. "I know, all those years ago, we said a lot of foolish things to each other. We were too young, really. Now that we've both seen a bit more of the world, it got me to wondering."

Her face was only a few inches from his. Lenny had forgotten how much he liked to be this close. He just had to lean forward, and they could kiss.

"And, uh," he said softly, "just what were you wondering?"

Her oh-so-kissable lips curled up into the slightest of smiles. She leaned forward.

Bum-bum-bum.

Someone knocked on the front door.

"Somebody you know?" Lenny asked Sheila.

She frowned. "I have no idea. I came up here alone."

Bum-bum-bum. The person outside knocked a second time. "Maybe I can get them to go away," Lenny said.

He looked through the spyhole in the door and saw only shadows. The light in the hall must have gone out again.

Bam-bam-bam! The knock was getting louder.

"Just a minute!" Lenny unlocked the deadbolts and opened the door as far as the security chain would allow.

Two men in trench coats stood outside. At least, Lenny thought, they were both male. They were tall with broad shoulders beneath the coats. But with the light out in the hallway, their faces were lost in shadow.

"Mr. Mumblemumble?" they both asked together.

"Pardon?" Lenny asked.

"Mumblemumble?" They repeated. Or maybe they had mumbled something entirely new. It was hard to tell.

"There's nobody with that name living here," Lenny answered, hoping it had something to do with what they just said.

The second one stepped forward, but didn't leave the shadows.

"Mr. Mumblemumble. Do you, by any chance, have a stamp collection?"

"Who are you?" Lenny demanded. This was an invasion of his private life. Especially now, with Sheila—well, that moment was probably lost forever. And how did they know about his stamps? It was just like Terrifitemps. Did everybody know everything about him now? "What do you want from me?"

The two stood there for a long moment, staring at him. At least he thought they were staring. It was pretty hard to tell what was going on with their faces lost in the gloom.

"Sorry," the one on the left finally spoke. "We must have the wrong place."

"Yeah," the one on the right echoed. "Wrong."

They both pivoted away at the same moment and, with only a step or two, vanished down the hall into the gloom. Lenny had never seen the hallway so dark before.

He stood there for a long moment, gazing into the gloom. The lightbulb above his doorway sputtered back to life. A couple more flickered back on farther down the corridor, then over the stairwell at the end of the corridor. All the lights that had been out flared back to life. The hallway seemed almost painfully bright. And completely empty.

Even though he hadn't heard them go down the stairs, Lenny saw no sign of the two who had stood there only a moment before.

Lenny stared at the silent hallway, then turned and closed the door. Who were those guys? Why had they shown up now? This could have absolutely nothing to do with the job. How could it?

"Uh, Sheila? I'm sorry about that. Who knows who those guys—"

He walked back into his apartment.

And froze.

He had left the loose-leaf notebooks in two neat piles. Now the half dozen notebooks had been scattered across the table. His pulse racing, he opened the notebook containing the heart of his collection, and quickly flipped the pages. He stopped and stared at the empty Mylar sleeve. Someone had taken his misprinted Moldavian first day cover! He could still see his missing treasure; an envelope issued on the day the stamp was made public, with the blue and red ink plates reversed, so that half the image was upside down!

Someone had been working with those strange people at the door, on the morning he was about to start a new job. He felt his right hand curl into a fist. His life might have been filled with poverty, boredom, and lack of female companionship, but, until now, he had his stamps!

And where was his ex-girlfriend? Had the strangers done something to her? Lenny stopped mid-room, his every sense alert.

He heard snoring. He looked to his right, and saw Sheila sound asleep on the couch.

He gently shook her shoulder.

"What?" She opened her eyes. "Lenny? You answered the door. Everything got foggy . . ." She leaped to her feet. "This is another one of those—things, isn't it? Like that rain of frogs at our Fourth of July picnic? Or the time that sinkhole swallowed my Toyota?" She looked straight at him, tears in her eyes. "I hoped you had outgrown that sort of thing! Now I remember why it all ended." She turned and grabbed her purse from the couch. "Good-bye, Lenny. I'm sorry I bothered you!"

She swept by him, out of his living room, out his front door, and out of his life.

Lenny found himself very much awake. In a matter of minutes, he had lost both his most valuable stamp and the girl he thought he'd lost years ago! Should he call the police? After what had happened, Lenny wasn't sure he could be coherent. And he couldn't be late on his first day of work! The call could wait, along with the coffee. He decided to get dressed and out of his apartment before anything else happened.

Lenny hadn't been out of his apartment this early in a long time.

The sun was bright, the air was crisp. And the subway was packed.

Lenny grabbed one of the straps and did his best not to fall into anybody's lap as the train barreled down the tracks.

He tried his best not to think of Sheila. Her visit felt more like a dream than anything real. So he thought about that missing first day cover instead.

Something that rare would be hard to sell. Once he'd reported it, every legitimate dealer in town would be on the lookout. Who were those strange people? Why had they stolen something that only really meant something to Lenny? How had they even known about his stamps? And why had they stolen it now?

Did it have anything to do with the new job? That was crazy talk. But why did he keep thinking that sort of thing over and over? Was he trying to sabotage himself before he even got started?

An image of Sheila asleep on the couch popped into his head; that moment when she was asleep on the couch, so pretty, so peaceful, as though that couch was where she belonged.

He looked up as the train pulled out of a station and realized his stop was next. Enough of stamps and Sheila. The morning rush hour seemed all too familiar. Once a commuter, always a commuter.

The train pulled into South Station and Lenny managed to extricate himself from the crowded car, following the moving throng toward the nearest escalator. He seemed to remember it being brighter down here. Shadows spread around the support columns. The sign for the donut stand in the corner barely flickered. The now departing train was the only source of light, its bright glow shrinking as it disappeared down the tunnel.

Lenny turned his head quickly. Was that a tall man in a raincoat stepping through the shadows? Lenny couldn't really see anything beyond the masses surging up the escalators and the stairs. Just his imagination. A lot of people wore raincoats. Why would someone follow him? Did they want something else from him? This couldn't have anything to do with Terrifitemps.

No one barred his way. No one even approached him. His feet found the first step of the escalator, and he rose toward the light of day. He stepped out onto the sunlit street, a world away from the murky depths of the subway. He had to forget about the theft, at least for the next few hours. He had a new job ahead of him.

"Lenny?"

He looked across the street. Sheila was waving at him. Maybe he should just wave back and keep on walking. The pedestrian walk light was on to the other side. His feet led him across without conscious thought.

Sheila's smile was more uncertain than before. "I'm sorry I stormed out on you like that. Somebody broke into your apartment. Why did I blame you?"

Lenny knew why. Odd things happened in his life. And, after that, really odd things followed. After a while, Sheila got annoyed. Twice. And, after a while more, she had left him. Also twice.

Sheila waved at the row of office buildings up the street. "I have an interview at Budwick, Budwick, Budwick and Klein. They're looking for a legal secretary."

"Uh, I have something new I'm starting," Lenny replied. "I don't know all that much about it yet."

"Really?" Sheila was her old bubbly self again. "I'm glad we bumped into each other again. "Maybe visiting you this morning was the right thing to do. Maybe it will bring me luck."

She gave him a quick kiss on the cheek. "I'll call you!"

Lenny stood and watched her walk away. Maybe Sheila was back in his life after all.

The bank clock on the corner told him it was 8:53. Maybe he had better get to work.

He moved quickly to the building that housed the temp agency, crossed the lobby, and jumped into a half-filled elevator that rose quickly to the fourteenth floor.

The doors opened. He was the only one getting off.

Lenny walked around the corner to the door he had used for his exit the day before. Two words had been painted on the frosted glass. no solicitors.

Lenny tried the handle but the door was locked. He saw a small button by the side of the door, with an even smaller sign: ring for entry. The door opened before Lenny could press the buzzer. The tall, sallow-skinned man from last Thursday stood on the other side.

"You are early."

Lenny glanced down at his cell phone. "Two minutes?"

"Still early. Karnowski never lies!"

"Don't pay too much attention to old Karny," a woman's voice called from somewhere deeper in the room. "He grows on you."

Lenny stepped past Karnowski to see that a small group of people stood behind the tall man. One of them was Ms. Siggenbottom, the austere woman who hired him. To one side of her stood a very thin man wearing very thick glasses, while on her other side Lenny's gaze was drawn to a striking young woman, not just for her artfully applied makeup and her long red hair, but her totally tight, totally black costume—suit, blouse, stockings, and sensible heels. She looked like she was dressed in business gothic.

"These are all members of your team," Ms. Siggenbottom began brusquely.

Team? Lenny almost said out loud.

"Karnowski he has met!" the tall man said with a deep breath of pride. "But he does not know my title. I am Karnowski the Ghost Finder!"

Ghost finder? Lenny swallowed those words as well.

The thin fellow stepped forward. He was wearing a heavy red sweater so bulky he seemed a bit like a turtle peaking out of his shell.

"You may call me Withers."

Lenny felt like he should say something. "And I'll be working with all of you?"

"All of them," Ms. Siggenbottom agreed. "And one more. There is a team member we can only meet after dark."

The others nodded as if this was only to be understood.

"But I have neglected to introduce our final member," the older woman continued. "The young woman is named Lenore."

The young woman stepped forward, her well-penciled brow creasing with effort. Lenny found her strangely attractive—where his old girlfriend was bright and bubbly, this Lenore had an air of the mysterious about her.

Her voice was a low whisper. "Say nothing."

Lenny swallowed his hello. Her pale-green eyes stared at his face with such intensity that Lenny felt she might see into his soul.

She spoke slowly, as if she had to search for every word. "You find me attractive—and dangerous."

Lenny frowned. She certainly was good-looking. Dangerous? Well, maybe. With all the black eyeliner, her face looked rather fierce.

She smiled slightly as she saw his reaction.

"You find everything strange. You're not entirely sure of Terrifitemps. Ms. Siggenbottom is an enigma."

Well, that was all true. Was she reading his mind? She was pretty good.

She took another step toward him, her dark-red lips turned with the slightest of smiles.

"And your name is—don't tell me—"

She paused for an instant before she announced: "Lance!"

Lenny shook his head.

"Leroy!"

Another shake.

"Sonny?" Her smile was wavering. She snapped her fingers. "I know!" She pointed straight at him.

"Hoppy!"

Hoppy? Maybe she wasn't quite as good as she thought.

"Lenny," he interjected helpfully.

"The very next name I was going to say!" Lenore cried triumphantly. "No man is a mystery to me."

"She wields an awesome power," Karnowski agreed. "At least some of the time."

Ms. Siggenbottom clapped her hands brusquely. "The introductions are over. We have more important matters to attend to!" She turned back to Lenny. "You will need some basic instruction."

Instruction in what? was the next thing Lenny didn't say. With this group, he guessed a few days as a file clerk were out of the question.

"And we have not discussed salary." She took a pen from the desk and wrote some numbers on the back of an envelope. "This should be your approximate take-home pay."

Lenny looked at the numbers as she handed him the envelope.

"Monthly?" he asked.

"Weekly," she replied.

The number was three times as much as Lenny had ever made, anywhere. For that much money, he would clean elephant cages.

Lenny nodded. "I'm in."

"I knew you would be." Ms. Siggenbottom clapped her hands again. "Now to work!"

Three

"So you're Lenny? Welcome to the team."

Lenny turned to see the skinny guy with the glasses and oversized sweater holding a hand out in his direction.

"Thanks." He took the other man's hand and shook it vigorously. He felt better already. Lenny hadn't realized how much he needed a smiling face.

"Everybody calls me Withers," the other man replied. "Trust me. You don't want to know my first name." He nodded at the dozen or so people milling about the room: "So what do you think of our little operation?"

Lenny tried to think of a polite way to express his feelings. "It's all a little overwhelming."

Withers chuckled. "I know just how you feel. When I first came here, I thought I had walked into a madhouse." He waved to the others Lenny had just met. "Everyone is quite committed to their jobs. They're all quite dependable, too. I'm sure you'll fit right in. It's just we all have—individual quirks."

Lenny looked past Withers at the very dramatic young woman talking to the very tall pale man. They were certainly both individuals. There were others, though, especially three short fellows with heavy beards over by the filing cabinets, who Lenny thought he might have trouble telling apart.

"I've found it quite pleasant to work here," Withers continued. "Even exciting. It is quite a learning experience."

Lenny turned back to the other man. He almost jumped when he saw Ms. Siggenbottom standing directly in front of them. It seemed as though she had just appeared there without having to do anything as inconvenient as walk.

"Come now, Mr. Withers," she said in her best disappointed-schoolteacher voice. "Your reports are due."

Withers smiled at her. "Duty calls." Withers waved to Lenny as he walked to his desk. "We can talk some more later."

Ms. Siggenbottom turned her laser gaze back on Lenny.

He actually smiled at her, too. With everything that had happened this morning, he had been feeling overwhelmed since he had walked through the door. Having someone like Withers to talk to made him feel better already. Once he got to know the others, he was sure he would feel just fine.

"And you!" Her voice suggested Lenny had already done something wrong. "It is time for the video."

Lenny felt the floor shift beneath his feet. Someone shouted. A jar full of pens crashed to the floor nearby.

"What was that?" Lenny asked in a voice just barely above a whisper.

Ms. Siggenbottom frowned. "Nothing that we have not dealt with before. You may be certain that the phenomenon does not extend beyond the inner office."

She looked to the man with glasses. "Withers? Do we have a report?"

He hustled back to their side, a large sheaf of papers in his hands. "The elves report unusually negative subnautaturgical energy."

Subnautaturgical? Lenny frowned. Elves? He guessed Withers was using some kind of company code for whatever had just happened.

The older woman nodded in satisfaction. "Exactly what we should expect. Continue with your earlier report, Mr. Withers." She looked around the room. "We should all get back to business."

She walked past Lenny and opened a door he hadn't seen before. He could feel the confusion taking over again. What else wasn't he seeing?

Lenny followed Ms. Siggenbottom into a room dominated by a very large TV. Actually, it was the cabinet housing the TV that was huge. The twenty-five-inch screen would have been state of the art thirty years ago. A half dozen plastic chairs were jammed into the remaining space.

"Sit," Ms. Siggenbottom commanded. Lenny sat.

She leaned forward and twisted a knob. A bright light appeared at the center of the screen, and—after a minute or so—turned into a snow-filled TV picture. She opened a cabinet door to the right of the screen. Behind it, Lenny saw a storage compartment with three shelves. She pulled a black plastic video box from the bottom shelf, extracted a tape, and inserted it into a top-loading video player sitting on the next shelf above. A label on the side of the player said it was a Betamax.

"There we go," she announced as she pressed a button on the player and turned to leave.

Well, at least they had some technology, Lenny thought as he waited for the show to begin. With everything he had seen around here, he was surprised they had a video player at all. But what had he expected? A slide show? Shadow puppets?

Lenny realized he was not alone. The chair next to him squeaked as it was dragged across the linoleum. The tall man smiled, showing far too many teeth, as he sat by Lenny's side.

"Karnowski cannot get enough of video!"

"Come and find me if you have any questions," Ms. Siggenbottom called out as she closed the door. The room grew dark as the screen filled with static.

Lenny jumped as the opening fanfare blasted from hidden speakers.

"Karnowski loves trumpets," his fellow employee agreed.

The static faded as the company logo spread across the screen.

"Terrifitemps," a deep, male voice announced. "Performing tomorrow's tasks today."

The screen was filled with a row of smiling cartoon men and women. All wore black T-shirts with TERRIFITEMPS! emblazoned in white across their cartoon chests.

The smiling figures, seven—no, eight of them—spread across the screen, each highlighted by a bold yellow circle. Lenny's attention darted from one cartoon character to the next as they sprang into action. One donned a construction hat, another walked into a rocket ship, another appeared to be aiming a gun at a dinosaur.

"So you are new here!" the video voice cried jovially. "Welcome to Terrifitemps! Welcome to a world of possibilities!"

The eight circles spun about each other. The jaunty music once again rose in the background until one of the circles grew to fill the screen. This particular cartoon employee was silhouetted in front of a full moon.

"Congratulations, new employees. And welcome to your new career in"—another fanfare—"Mystical Sciences!

"In the next few days, you will embark on a bold new adventure as you combine our special training with those unique skills that led us to hire you. Before you know it, you'll become a Total Terrifitemp!"

Lenny started as someone shrieked in the other room. He turned to Karnowski.

"Is only Withers," the tall man spoke quietly at his side. "Karnowski pays no attention."

Withers? The only person who appeared normal in this place? Lenny was half out of his plastic chair before he was aware of moving. Shouldn't they do something?

But Karnowski did not seem bothered. Maybe people shrieked all the time around here. Maybe this was some of the excitement the thin man with glasses had been talking about.

Lenny turned back to the video.

"Let us take you through a typical day on your new job—or should I say typical night? What do you see?"

The TV screen filled with the image of a moonlit field. Bats flew over a round, yellow shape in the sky.

"Strange shadows, sinister shapes crossing the moon, odd noises in the night. Why should we care? Terrifitemps is there!"

A spotlight roved the landscape, stopping abruptly to illuminate a shrieking mass of eyes and claws and teeth. They were still cartoons, but they weren't cute.

"Terrifitemps will give you the knowledge to deal with"—the voice chuckled—"well, just about anything!"

As the narrator spoke, the eyes, claws, and teeth were snared in a glowing net. "You'll also be trained to use our special equipment—"

Another shriek, louder this time, came from the other side of the wall.

"Withers?" Lenny asked.

Karnowski glanced back at the outer office. "Has trouble with full moon. Video explains everything."

"With your training, beasties beware!" the video voice continued. "Ghoulies will be gone. And absolutely nothing will go bump in the night!"

More trumpets.

"Terrifitemps. Keeping the world safe for everybody else! Let's begin your training!"

A chalkboard appeared on the screen. the first lesson was written on the board by an invisible hand.

"And now," the voice continued. "Lesson one, the most important lesson of all. Pay close attention. Your life may depend on it!"

Out in the main office, the banging and shrieking began again, so loud now that it almost drowned out the next fanfare. To Lenny, it sounded like a bad action movie was filming right next door.

The tall man frowned. "For this, even Karnowski must pause video." He jumped up and hit a button on the VCR, then crossed to the door. For a large man, he was very quick. Lenny was right behind him.

The office next door was in chaos. Everyone was moving in every possible direction. Papers were flying through the air. Every rotary phone was ringing nonstop. And above all that racket, someone was squealing.

Someone, or something.

"Oh my god! What is that?" The words escaped his lips almost before he thought them. Lenny found himself staring at the world's largest rat, or squirrel, or something. It was definitely a gray-furred rodent that was definitely six feet tall. It darted back and forth, now on top of a desk, now under another, as people tried to grab it with nets and hooks and hands.

"Is Withers," Karnowski said. "But change does not happen until nightfall!"

"Usually," Lenore replied as she stepped past Lenny. "Unless other forces come into play."

Karnowski looked horrified. "Do you mean?"

"I'm afraid so."

Everybody in the office (except the giant rodent) nodded as one.

Lenore excused herself and moved into the crowd as Withers jumped into a corner. He seemed to have calmed a bit. His pink nose twitched furiously as he carefully watched everyone around him.

Employees stepped out of the way as Ms. Siggenbottom strode across the room. She was headed straight for Lenny. "It is very fortunate you came today. We need all of your skills for what will come."

Lenore emerged from the crowd. "I've got the gun."

Lenny heard a muffled bang. A red-feathered dart stuck out of Wither's hindquarters. The crowd hastily retreated as the giant rodent crashed to the floor. The very large mousey thing began to snore.

Lenny took a cautious step forward to get a closer look at the now sleeping beast. "This is Withers?"

Lenore nodded with a frown. "He's a werevole."

"His skills are somewhat more limited than yours," Ms. Siggenbottom added.

"And what skills are those?" Lenny asked, not sure that he wanted to know.

"He has great tunneling ability, for one," Ms. Siggenbottom replied.

"And?" Lenny broke through the silence that followed.

"Generally," Lenore added, "the moment people see him, they scream 'Oh my god! What is that?'"

"It provides us the opportunity to do whatever is necessary," Ms. Siggenbottom continued. "A bit limited perhaps, but very useful."

Lenny still didn't get it. "So he always runs around and screams like that?"

Ms. Siggenbottom sniffed, as if that was the most foolish question she had ever heard. "Certainly not. He has far more control when his transformation is more—normal."

Lenny watched as a couple of men propped the giant rodent onto a hand cart and wheeled him from the room. What was normal about a werevole?

"This was somewhat more dramatic than our last incident." Ms. Siggenbottom's frown deepened more than usual. "But we have dealt with problems like this before. I am afraid your training will need to be accelerated."

"Do I finish watching the video?" Lenny took a step back toward the viewing room.

"No time," she replied. "From here out, you are learning everything on the job."

"We'll all pitch in," Lenore agreed, waving her gun. "Worst-case scenario, we blow things up."

"Great teachers!" Karnowski agreed, pounding on his chest. "With luck, you learn great deal before you are killed!"

Ms. Siggenbottom glanced at her jewel-encrusted wristwatch. "Situation meeting in twenty minutes! Move people, or we will meet a fate like Withers!"

Four

The three short, hairy fellows began moving desks. Karnowski and Lenore started stacking plastic chairs. Everyone in the room was on the move—everyone but Lenny. With Withers out of the picture, Lenny didn't just not know who to talk to—he didn't know what he should do.

"Is very exciting, yes?" Karnowski appeared by Lenny's side. "Karnowski remembers his first emergency! Run screaming, great panic, bloody death around corner! Very exciting!"

Great panic? Bloody death? There was a lot more going on here than a missing first day cover. Lenny wondered if he could still change his mind about this whole job thing.

Ms. Siggenbottom pulled out a large ring of keys and locked the door that led to the lobby.

Lenore paused directly in front of him and stared into his eyes. Once again, he felt as if her penetrating, green-eyed gaze could see into his very soul. "Odd that this should happen now, just when you've joined the team." She pursed her red lips. "You didn't talk to anybody who was"—her well-plucked brows furrowed in concentration—"uh, difficult to see?"

Lenny thought of the figures in the shadows outside his door. Did she already know? Especially if she could see into his soul? But even if she knew, what did it mean?

"Difficult to see?' Ms. Siggenbottom tut-tutted at Lenore's side. "She speaks of the Dimm, one of many groups whose goals are – different from our own. Actually, it is not odd at all that this should happen at precisely this moment, as you all will discover. Follow me."

Lenore stepped to Lenny's side as they followed the older woman. "You do have one very grave problem. Every time I look at you, I keep seeing—postage stamps."

She looked away before Lenny could explain. Lenny wondered if she could sense anything about Sheila, too. Now why should that bother him?

Ms. Siggenbottom walked to the room's nearest corner and nodded her head. Karnowski picked up a large, Chinese-style vase from the table there, revealing a large red button on the wall; a button pressed by Ms. Siggenbottom.

Lenny heard a deep rumbling sound, as though the subway was running on the next floor down. Walls slid away to reveal a great hall with a vaulted ceiling. The room was lined on either side with those huge computers Lenny remembered from 1950s science fiction films, the kind with lots of blinking lights and reel-to-reel tape decks. A long table of polished blond wood dominated the center of the room. It was surrounded by plenty of plastic chairs.

At least twenty other individuals had gathered at the far end of the room. Some of them did not look human.

Lenny's attention was caught by a bright-orange handle on a rod that protruded from the wall just beyond the newly created opening to the hall. Immediately above this rod hung a large placard, maybe four feet by six, with foot-high glowing red letters that read DO NOT TOUCH THIS LEVER!

"If I might have your attention."

Ms. Siggenbottom's commanding voice cut through the confusion. Everyone paused to look in her direction.

She had traveled to the far end of the table while Lenny had been gaping in wonder. She stood now between a much-too-tall green fellow and what appeared to be a purple squid wearing a diver's helmet.

She cleared her throat. Everyone hastily took a seat, Lenny included.

"Welcome to the Eastern U.S. headquarters of Terrifitemps International. Thank you all for assembling on such short notice. Events have taken a dramatic turn, as we have been expecting."

She paused to look directly across the table.

"Before I go any further, I need to introduce our newest Terrifitemp. We usually like to bring in our new recruits slowly, but current circumstances prevent this. We expect great things of this young man. May I present Lenny Hodge."

A great rumble filled the room.

"Hi, Lenny!" the rumble said.

Lenny stood there, mesmerized by the sound of his name. That, and he thought he could watch the purple squid undulate for hours.

The room fell silent. He realized he was expected to respond.

"Hi, everybody!" he called back. His voice seemed to get lost in the room's vastness. He raised his right hand in a half-hearted wave.

"And now, our situation," Ms. Siggenbottom's clear voice began again. "I will review matters quickly, so that both those old and new might understand.

"This is the day we have been preparing for. We know there are some who—oppose us. We have had two—incidents—already during the past week, one mere hours ago. An organization as powerful as Terrifitemps is bound to make enemies. And we have more than one.

"They go by many names. The Old Ones. The Teenie Weenies. Those Hideous Things No One Wants to Talk About. Evil Industries, Inc. S.M.U.R.S.H. And, of course, certain branches of the phone company."

She paused to survey the room. "But why do they attack us now? There could be many reasons, and I am sure we will uncover all of them eventually through our investigations. But I suspect one of the primary reasons rests with our newest employee, the young man who you have just met."

Every head in the room swiveled in Lenny's direction. Lenny fought a sudden urge to hide under the table. What was Ms. Siggenbottom saying? The tremor happened because he was standing here? It was because of Lenny that Withers had turned into an oversized squirrel?

"Why is our Mr. Hodge so special?" the director asked. "He does not look special. Compared to many of us, he looks quite ordinary. He possesses absolutely no qualities to distinguish him from the crowd. He might pass you by on the street without you being aware of his existence."

The assembled masses studied Lenny with deep frowns on their faces, as though they were judging him and finding him less than adequate.

Ms. Siggenbottom kept on talking. "All of that does not matter. It is not so much who Mr. Hodge is, or what he looks like, but what he can do."

Lenny was suddenly very aware of Lenore. She stared at him from her seat to his left, her eyes boring their way into his skull—as though she already knew what the heck Ms. Siggenbottom was going to say.

"Mr. Hodge," the older woman said. "You have the advantage over many of those seated here today. For a rank beginner, you have a lot of experience. For example—" She paused to smile at her audience. "We know how you survived that bizarre lemming migration outside of Minneapolis."

The lemmings? Lenny had nearly forgotten about them. And all that time, he was supposed to be in St. Paul.

"Events like that do not happen to everyone," their leader continued. "In fact, they hardly happen to anyone at all. Except for you, Mr. Hodge."

She pointed at Lenny. "You do remember encountering those dancing mole creatures in the Mississippi Delta? Performing Swan Lake?"

Well, of course he did. But what of it? Anybody could have seen that. He just happened to be standing there when it happened.

"You just happened to be in the right place," Ms. Siggenbottom agreed. Lenny looked quickly at Lenore. Did everybody know what he was thinking?

"I hardly have to mention that waterspout off the coast of France," the older woman added.

Lenny's mouth fell open. Until now, he had been sure that mermaid had been his imagination. A chill passed through him. Maybe there was something to what Ms. Siggenbottom was saying.

"We don't have time to delve into any of the many, many other amazing occurrences. You have had a very active life, Mr. Hodge. If you have ever thought about it."

Thought about it? Lenny didn't, all that much. He was always worried about making a little money, or whether or not he would ever get a steady girlfriend. Whenever his life got really bad, he would shut out the world and work on his stamp collection. And now, even his stamps had suffered! Things always did happen around him. Maybe not thinking about it (stamps included) was nothing more than a defense mechanism.

"It is a strange gift, Mr. Hodge," Ms. Siggenbottom agreed. "It could even make a person go crazy—unless there were a very good reason for it."

Lenny nodded. A very good reason? He would certainly like to hear it.

"Many of those in this room make things happen, Mr. Hodge. But you are the only one, to my knowledge, that has things happen all around him, all the time. There are those among us who can call thunder and lightning from the sky. But only you, Mr. Hodge, by your very being, can cause the lightning to come to him.

"Things happen everywhere, every day, Mr. Hodge. But you are a one-person human happening, and everything we need to happen will happen to you! With you in our employ, Mr. Hodge, Terrifitemps will triumph!"

Lenny heard shouts and cheers. Everyone around the table rose together to give him a standing ovation.

Lenny guessed that meant he really couldn't leave.

Ms. Siggenbottom stopped clapping. The rest of the audience stopped an instant later.

"I know that this is a lot of information for you to process, Mr. Hodge.

You have only now become aware of your abilities. You will only be able to learn to use them through experience. That is why I have assigned you to our most experienced team of agents. We are, unfortunately, minus one of their number already. But with you on the team, I'm sure your teammates' fortunes, and indeed the prospects of all of Terrifitemps, will improve immensely."

They would? If Ms. Siggenbottom didn't intimidate Lenny quite so much, he might have asked her how he was supposed to do that sort of thing. Not that he even knew what he meant by "that sort of thing."

"Very good," Ms. Siggenbottom added when it was apparent that Lenny had nothing to say. "You will be under the command of Mr. Karnowski. Follow his lead, and I am sure you will do very well indeed." She clapped her hands. "Now the rest of us must get back to work!"

Well, Lenny thought, at least now he knew what he was expected to do. At least after a fashion. He followed Karnowski and Lenore out of the room.

They had not walked ten feet before they heard another blood-curdling scream. All three of them turned back to the office they had just left. The scream had come from somewhere inside.

"Withers again?" Lenny asked.

Lenore shook her head. "That scream came from someone more powerful than Withers." She turned and ran back to the other room. Lenny followed as quickly as he could.

As soon as Lenny stepped back through the door, he saw exactly what Lenore had been talking about.

Ms. Siggenbottom now stood on top of a desk at the room's center. She had a wild look in her eyes, far different from her usual strict composure. The employees crowded around the desk had all taken a step back, as if to give their director extra room.

Ms. Siggenbottom looked straight at Lenny and his team. She announced, in a clear and commanding voice:

"Giant economy corn dog!"

"What?" the pale man said at his side. "Karnowski does not—"

"Giant!" Ms. Siggenbottom's voice rose close to a scream. "Economy! Corn! Dog!"

"She's having trouble speaking," Lenore explained with her usual frown. "Something is interfering with her voice—no—her ability to communicate."

The director pointed at Lenore and shook her head vigorously. "Giant economy corn dog!" Her brow furrowed, as if she was doing her utmost to concentrate. "Giant!" She bit her lip, and took a deep breath. "Economy giant dog corn!"

Karnowski looked grimmer than usual. "Everything else this morning may have happened before. This, Karnowski believes, is new."

"Corn dog!" Ms. Siggenbottom screamed in agreement.

"Lenny!" Lenore cried over her shoulder as she rushed to their boss's side. "Stay close! Perhaps together we can use our powers to restore Ms. Siggenbottom!"

Lenore gripped both of the director's shoulders and stared deep into her eyes. "Ms. Siggenbottom! Speak to me!"

"Giant—" the older woman began.

"No!" Lenore commanded. "Those are only words! Reach past them, and speak!

"I—Oh—Eeee—" Ms. Siggenbottom began to tremble. "Shrah—shrin—shrink swelling in your mucous membrane!" She shook her head. "Membrane! Mucous mucous!"

"I do not believe this is progress," Karnowski murmured darkly. "What does Lenore see?"

"I believe there are darker things, lurking beneath," the young woman replied, her forehead creased in concentration. "But in her conscious mind, nothing but corn dogs."

"Lenny!" the younger woman called. "Take my hand! Together, we can bring her back!"

Lenny took Lenore's outstretched hand. Her fingers were cool to the touch. "Ms. Siggenbottom! We're here to help! Look at us! What do you want to say?"

"Mucous? Corn dog?" She shook her head violently. She tried to smile past her spasms. "Fa-fa-fa-fun for the whole family!"

Karnowski caught her before she fell to the ground.

Lenny felt a buzzing against his thigh. He had set his phone on vibrate. He couldn't look away from the scene before him. Lenore and Karnowski both hovered over the unconscious Ms. Siggenbottom, while a dozen other employees rushed to and fro on errands Lenny couldn't possibly imagine.

It was not the best time to get a call.

Five

Lenny stared as a pair of over muscled men hustled their employer out of the conference room. With Ms. Siggenbottom gone, most of the noise left the room as well.

Lenny finally pulled his phone from his pocket. He had missed a call—from Sheila! Apparently she was determined to see him again. But when could he actually get away from here? Despite all the corn dogs and mucous membranes, the now unconscious Ms. Siggenbottom had been right. Things always happened to Lenny. But even he couldn't remember them happening this fast.

The tall man pulled a watch from the pocket of his vest. "Karnowski cannot delay! We must go to our—other location."

"There are other parts of Terrifitemps?" Lenny asked.

Lenore nodded. "More than any one of us knows." She glanced at her own phone. "But look at the time. It's well past lunch, closer to dinner really. We need to get some supplies before we travel."

"Karnowski says eat on the run!" the ghost finder agreed.

Lenore led them to the back of the room, opening the door to a much smaller room beyond—a room that held a few small tables and a pair of vending machines.

"Karnowski says they need to stock these more often!"

Lenny could see exactly what the other man meant. The soda machine had half a dozen choices, all but one of which had a red "out" light above the name. Lenny put in some quarters and pushed the last remaining choice. He studied the can. He hadn't even known they still made grape Nehi soda.

The other machine displayed shelf after shelf of prepared food, except all but two of the display rows were empty as well. One row showed three pale-white sandwiches. The other showed something blue and green and lumpy, as though whatever had once been there had long ago surrendered to mold and mildew.

"What's that?" Lenny asked.

"Nothing for humans," Karnowski grumbled.

"Nothing for what?" Lenny asked.

"These machines have to provide sustenance to everyone," Lenore began. She looked at the green moldy thing. "We'll have to explain that later."

"Is sandwiches for Karnowski." He inserted a bill into the machine's cash slot and pressed a row of buttons. Three of the pale sandwiches slid to the bottom of the chute.

"Cream cheese and olive. No crust. Very refined."

Lenny unwrapped the cellophane and took a taste. He supposed they were edible. But not much more.

"When Ms. Siggenbottom not hungry, they stay in machine forever," Karnowski added.

Lenny had never been so grateful for the taste of grape Nehi.

"But we must go," the ghost finder said after finishing his sandwich in three bites. He took a step back into the larger room. Lenny finished the last of the soda and left the rest behind as he and Lenore followed Karnowski.

Karnowski pushed the stem on his watch and a row of bookcases moved aside, revealing the battered green door of an ancient elevator. Lenny wondered if there were any walls in this office that didn't hide something.

"Much is always hidden from view," Lenore intoned.

Karnowski stepped forward. "Going down!" The aged metal doors opened with a groan, revealing a metal grate. Karnowski pulled the grate aside and the three of them walked in. Lenny saw that the controls consisted of six mahogany-brown buttons. Even though they, too, were worn with age, he could faintly discern the labels B1 through B6.

"We're going all the way down, aren't we?" Lenny asked. Karnowski nodded as the elevator lurched into action.

Lenny was beginning to get the hang of this.

The ancient elevator shuddered to a halt at B6—the bottom floor. Karnowski led them out into a dimly lit hallway, then, three doors down, into an even more dimly lit room. Once Lenny's eyes got accustomed to the light from the single overhead bulb, he saw that the room was empty, except for four coffins leaning against the far wall.

Lenore frowned back at Karnowski. "Isn't it time?"

The tall man consulted his watch. "Half an hour past."

Lenore sighed as she walked up to the second coffin from the left. "I guess I'll have to knock."

Lenny wondered if he could wait in the other room—any other room. But he took a deep breath and stood absolutely still as Lenore strode forward to bang on the coffin lid.

Nothing happened. Lenny started breathing again.

Lenore was not happy. She had knocked twice on the largest of the four coffins, the noise echoing around the cavernous room. She pulled her arm back and really pounded on the lid.

"Who disturbs my eternal rest?" a voice rumbled at last from deep within.

Lenore was unfazed. "Can it, Herbert. You've got to go to work like the rest of us."

The coffin lid opened slowly to reveal a man in an old-fashioned tux, his hands folded across his chest. The man's face was very pale, with the slightest indentations in his lower lip where the tips of two very pointy teeth peaked from beneath his upper lip.

Lenny had watched enough horror movies to know just what was going on. He already knew were-creatures and ghosts were part of the Terrifitemps team. Why not vampires? Especially vampires who could make coffin lids swing upward without moving their hands?

The hinged lid stopped with a groan once it had swung aside, and the man stepped from the box with a heavy sigh.

He surveyed the room as if it were every bit as disappointing as he had imagined.

"Where's the romance?" he moaned.

As if on cue, two of the other three coffins popped open. A woman stepped from each—their skin unusually pale, their lips an unnatural red. Their long hair cascaded across their bare shoulders; one the lightest shade of blonde, the other the deepest shade of black. Each wore a slightly tattered ball gown; the blonde wore rose, the brunette wore violet. But it was what was beneath those ball gowns that Lenny found fascinating. They both had what used to be called hourglass figures. Impossibly small waists, full, supple hips—and the cleavage, full, rounded globes nearly spilling out of the low-cut evening wear.

Lenny had never found cleavage quite so fascinating. He took a step forward with no conscious thought, as though he were being controlled by a will greater than his own. He dragged his gaze upward, away from the chests to the faces. They were both stunningly attractive, a cross between every prom queen, pop star, and fashion-magazine cover girl that Lenny had ever been drawn to. He took another step.

Vampires, he told himself. It was time to stop walking.

Both women smiled. They had beautiful smiles. You will come to me now, the smiles said.

Lenny couldn't look away. He stumbled forward. Vampires, he reminded himself again. Pointy teeth, sucking blood, living dead vampires. The woman in violet extended a slim, pale hand in his direction. He needed to touch that porcelain skin. His brain might scream no, but his shuffling feet said yes, yes, yes.

What else could Lenny think about? Something, anything!

Well, there was that fourth coffin. Three vampires already stood before him. What hideous thing lurked behind that closed lid?

The woman in rose smiled back at him. "New blood?"

Lenore stepped in front of Lenny, blocking his view of both vampire beauties.

"Ladies, I'm afraid he's part of the team."

Lenny shivered. His feet stopped moving. He remembered to breathe. He had wanted to get very close to those women very quickly. And—according to all those movies—he would have ended up very dead.

"Does anybody show up here who isn't a team member?" the vampire in violet complained. It was her turn to sigh. "Another night without a decent meal." She glared at the male vampire. "It was different, long ago..."

"Isn't that just like him?" the rose vampire agreed, staring at the Baron. "When you first meet, it's all fangs and candlelight. And then once he gets you home..."

Both fanged females snorted derisively.

"Brittany. Taylor," the male vampire chided, looking first at the blonde, then the brunette. "We can discuss this another time." He turned back to Lenny and the others. "You may call me—the Baron."

"The Baron is final member of our team," Karnowski explained.

"A mere member?" The Baron might have sneered. It was hard to tell with the fangs. "Would the team exist without my skills?"

The vampire women laughed, a sound as cold as winter wind. The Baron seemed not to notice.

Lenny's brain—once again his own—kept trying to find positives.

Ghost hunter, psychic, werebeast, vampire—that pretty much covered all the bases. And these creatures were his co-workers, after all. Better to have them with you than against you, right? His gaze wandered back to the closed coffin.

"We mostly do night work," Karnowski explained, perhaps unnecessarily.

"Herbert," Lenore said to the Baron. "We have a situation here." She briefly told him about Wither's unfortunate conversion.

The Baron grimaced, showing far more of his fangs than he had before. "This is what happens when I am not available. They've transformed him during the day?"

Lenore nodded. "We don't know how they did it. We have no idea even who did it. We have to suspect them all. But there's more." She quickly went on to describe Ms. Siggenbottom and the corn dogs.

The vampire's eyebrows rose in excited alarm. "It's about time our team had a real challenge!" His pale hand clenched into a fist as his blood-red eyes looked to the ceiling. "We will finally have a chance to test our true power! The Baron will triumph again!"

"Ooh, the big bad vampire!" Brittany cooed. "Why can't we see more of that at home?"

"How long has it been since we've had any real excitement?" Taylor chimed in. "It's just been one long, endless night!"

"I should have listened to my mother!" Brittany agreed. "You know what she always said: Why should a vampire buy the cow when he can suck its blood for free?"

The fourth coffin groaned and shifted against the wall, as if someone—or something—inside was looking for a way out. The Baron pointedly looked away from the still-closed box. He cleared his throat, shifting his cape awkwardly across his shoulders. "We should be going."

"You're going out in that cape?" Brittany called. "It looks like you've been sleeping in it!"

"If you'll pardon me?" The vampire moved out of the room at amazing speed. Lenny quickly followed before the two other vampires could look his way. The Baron slammed the door as soon as Lenore and Karnowski had joined them in the hall.

"Do you know how difficult it is to find an open dry cleaner's in the middle of the night?" the vampire muttered. "Perhaps I should start meeting you upstairs."

Lenore studied the undead fellow. "You would actually get out of your coffin if I didn't show up to knock?"

The vampire shrugged his caped shoulders. "A fellow's got to eat."

Lenore nodded. "But mostly he's got to sleep."

The vampire placed a pale hand on his chest. "You pierce me to the heart."

Lenore's shapely left eyebrow rose in disdain.

"Hey, you're the one with the fangs."

The vampire stared at Lenore, the slightest of smiles playing about his fangs. "When you torment me this way, I find you—strangely attractive."

Lenore quickly moved to the other side of Lenny. "Business, Herbert."

The Baron nodded as though all the joy had been drained from his existence. "Business."

An awkward silence descended over the group.

Lenny supposed, according to the rules, he was supposed to say something. "What do we do now?"

Karnowski nodded solemnly. "Karnowski has strict instructions from Ms. Siggenbottom—before she spoke of corn dogs. We take fight to them."

"And how do we do that?" Lenore asked next.

"You obviously need my sage advice." The Baron stepped forward. Away from his women, he seemed far more animated. "I can fly over the city looking for clues. Lenore can use her psychic powers. Karnowski can quiz his many ghostly informants."

Karnowski raised his hand for silence. "None of that will work. According to Ms. Siggenbottom, Lenny must lead the way."

"Really?" The Baron regarded Lenny with perhaps a bit too much attention. "Our new recruit becomes more interesting by the moment."

"Of course!" Lenore looked at Lenny with an alarming intensity. "You know things you do not realize. And we will have to discover every one of them, before what happened to Withers and Ms. Siggenbottom overcomes us all."

A part of Lenny wanted to object to this whole conversation. But how could he argue about something he—by definition—couldn't know? He decided he might as well start walking.

"The night calls me!" the Baron added enthusiastically as he fell in behind Lenny's lead. "I need to get out in the open air."

Lenny agreed. He found this sub-basement oppressive. He tried to think how he had felt in the past, just before he had encountered runaway meteors or herds of lemmings. A tingling in his toes? A strange foreboding? He remembered, just before he met that mermaid, he had been thinking how much he was in the mood for tacos. If he could just isolate that feeling again . . .

He stopped in front of a door with a sign that read authorized personnel only.

"We go in here," he announced to his own surprise.

Six

"Huh. Karnowski has never noticed this door before."

"None of us have," Lenore remarked with great portent. She tried the knob. It didn't budge.

"If I may?" The Baron stepped forward and leaned against the door. It opened with a loud clang and the sound of rending metal. "This is why you need a vampire, despite what certain females say."

Lenore did not seem impressed. "Lenny, if you would?"

Really? It was one thing to discover doors, another thing entirely to lead the way through to whatever was on the other side of them. But he was part of a team now. Everybody else knew what they were doing. He could pretend that he knew what was doing, too.

He led the way again, walking into a long, straight access tunnel built with gray cinder-block walls. Small lights, suspended from the ceiling every twenty feet or so, barely illuminated a painted yellow line that led down the middle of the floor.

Ending where? Lenny wondered. He guessed they were no longer under the building that housed Terrifitemps. Heck, they were probably no longer on the same city block. Did these tunnels parallel the subway? Or maybe they followed some ancient drainage system, or accessed some underground cables. Would the others know any more?

"A minute," Karnowski said just behind his shoulder. Lenny looked back at the tall, skeletal fellow, who nodded his head solemnly. "There are no ghosts here."

"I sense no creatures," the Baron added, "living or otherwise."

Lenore paused a moment before she, too, replied. "My readings are mixed, but I sense no immediate danger."

None of those answers matched Lenny's questions. "Does anyone know where we're going?" he asked.

The others paused for a moment before the tall man announced:

"Karnowski says to go forward!"

"Trust Ms. Siggenbottom," the vampire agreed as he waved for Lenny to once again lead the way.

Lenny guessed the answer to his question was "no." Still, the others had all done this sort of thing before. And something horrible had happened to Ms. Siggenbottom. And they were paying him a lot of money.

Lenny led the way again. The tunnel changed as they proceeded. And not in a good way. Cinder blocks gave way to faded bricks that leaked moisture, creating patches of moss on the walls and small puddles on the floor. The lights became smaller and less frequent, with the occasional bulb burned out, leaving them in almost total darkness. Who would change lightbulbs in a place like this, anyway? Lenny decided he didn't want to know the answer.

And besides, they had come to a wide spot in the passageway, large enough for them to stand side by side. And on the far wall of the wide space in the hall was a second, very large door.

Karnowski pushed against the shining steel plate. The door filled the wall floor to ceiling, as if it might open on a garage or a loading dock. It looked particularly formidable, a solid sheet of steel with rivets forming an X pattern from the corners to the center of the plate.

The door didn't budge.

"Is locked," Karnowski said with a grunt.

Lenny was not at all surprised. It was the sort of door that looked like it had to be totally impassable. All that steel, all those bolts.

The Baron stepped forward. "Let a vampire do his job." He pushed against the steel with his supernatural strength. And pulled. And strained. And grimaced. And grunted. Lenny began to wonder if a vampire could sweat.

The door still didn't budge.

"Except when the vampire isn't up to it," Lenore remarked with the slightest twitch of her ever-expressive eyebrows.

"Is locked," Karnowski confirmed.

Lenny felt a tap on his shoulder. He looked behind him to see a half-hidden recess, lost in shadow. Had one of his team members walked behind him? He looked back and saw that all three of them were crowded at the far end of the hall, staring at the door.

A hand grabbed his elbow and tugged him quite forcefully back into the recess.

Lenny found himself facing a man wearing a mask that might once have been white. The man pulled Lenny close. The masked man's breath smelled of onions.

"Thank goodness!" he whispered. "I caught you before it's too late!"

Lenny wondered if he should call out to the others. Not that this frantic man seemed to be much of a threat. And Lenny was supposed to be the whole reason these surprises happened, wasn't he? In his new life, masked people appearing out of nowhere was probably normal.

He took a step back to get a better look. The fellow wore a white jumpsuit with red and blue piping. His head was covered with a matching face mask. If Lenny were in a movie, this fellow's clothing might pass for a very worn superhero costume. But in the real world it looked like something Evel Knieval would wear right after he missed a jump with his motorcycle. Maybe Lenny should call the others after all.

"Excuse me," Lenny began. "I don't—"

"You are constantly confronted with the unusual, the unexplained," the man hurriedly replied in the same hushed tone. "Is this any different?"

"Well . . ." Lenny tried to think.

The other man nodded as though Lenny had answered his question. "I have been associated with Terrifitemps in the past. Now, with the unfortunate turn of events concerning Ms. Siggenbottom, it is time for me to return. After all, someone has to tell you what's really happening!"

They do? Lenny thought. It seemed every time someone explained the situation, he only ended up more confused.

The rumpled and masked man continued before Lenny could say anything at all. "You face great evil. You are up against the minions of Foo—an international mastermind of menace. Only so horrible an enemy is truly worthy of Terrifitemps. And others—including your Terrifitemps team—are watching your every move. You have the skills, even though you are only beginning to learn to use them. You are the leader. You are their only real hope. They need you to show them the way."

Lenny glanced quickly back at the others. The three of them had gathered around the door and were arguing loudly about the best way to open it by combining a vampire's strength, the possible aid of a ghost or two, and whatever psychic thing Lenore might manage. So much for watching his every move.

"You are new at this," the masked man continued. "It is natural to be tentative." He pushed a single gloved, smudged index finger against

Lenny's chest. "But you must put caution behind you."

"I must?"

"It's what Ms. Siggenbottom would want for you."

Well. Yeah, Lenny thought, that was more or less what Ms. Siggenbottom herself had said. It was better to have a sense of purpose.

The stranger nodded. "I know you'll find your way." He turned away.

It was Lenny's turn to reach out to the stranger. "We can use any help we can get. Why don't you come out—"

The other shook his head. "It is best that I only talk to you for now." He waved dismissively at the hallway beyond. "They are not ready for the truth!"

He took another step away. Lenny needed answers!

"Who are you, anyway?"

The masked man hesitated for a moment before he replied. "You can call me 'S.'"

"S?"

The other voices drifted in from the larger corridor. The Baron was pointing out how it didn't matter if Lenore could see past the door if they couldn't find any way to open it.

"More or less." S stepped farther back into the gloom. Something creaked behind him. "You are the leader now. I'll talk to you when I can."

Lenny took a step toward him, but saw only the faint outline of a door swinging shut in the wall.

S was gone.

Lenny stared at the darkness. He would take control—just what Ms. Siggenbottom had wanted. What did he have to lose? Sure, this S guy was a little strange. But was there anybody around here who wasn't mysterious?

He turned back toward his companions. Maybe he'd tell them what had just happened. Lenore and the Baron stared at each other, much like they had done before Lenny met S.

"I have ages of experience. A vampire knows far more than you."

"And is any of that knowledge useful in the real world?"

Then again, maybe he wouldn't tell them anything. Apparently the three of them were so busy arguing, none of them noticed he had been gone.

"Excuse me," he began.

The Baron gave Lenny the briefest of glances. "You have chosen to join the discussion? I had almost forgotten you were here. Perhaps I was too hasty in my faith in Ms. Siggenbottom."

"Job to do!" Karnowski barked. "Lenny reminds us!"

"There has to be some way to open this," Lenore said as she stepped forward to take a closer look. "Maybe if you hit the bolts in a specific pattern."

Lenny leaned forward to look over her shoulder. She poked at a few random bolts. Nothing happened. She poked them more vigorously. Still nothing.

Lenore frowned. "There's no way through."

They seemed to have forgotten about him all over again. Lenny would show them. S would be proud.

"Why don't we go this way?" Lenny piped up from the back.

The other three turned around to look at him.

"And what way would that be?" the Baron asked, arching a single brow.

"Follow me," he said as he turned back into the shadows. The door was right where he thought it would be. He had a moment of doubt as he pushed it open. What did he really know about this S fellow, anyway? He could be leading them into a trap. Lenny decided if he could cut through a bit of the Baron's smugness, it might be worth it.

"Wait!" Lenore announced. "Someone has been . . . nearby!"

"Was not ghost," Karnowski replied with a frown.

"Possibly human," the Baron added with distaste. "Too many onions."

The three of them crowded after Lenny through the door. He couldn't see a thing.

"It is a small room," the Baron declared. "It has a few—poles in one corner."

"My powers discern"—Lenore paused—"a light switch."

A single lightbulb flared overhead.

Karnowski was the first to say it. "Is broom closet."

The poles piled in one corner were actually broom and mop handles. The wooden floor was scuffed, and dull-gray paint peeled from the walls. Directly in front of them was a normal-looking door—with a brass doorknob.

"Seems safe enough," Lenore said as she gripped the knob with her right hand. "This door is unlocked. Let's see what this was meant to clean."

Lenny followed the others through the door.

"Is interesting at last," Karnowski admitted.

Lenny guessed that was one word for this. He thought the hidden door would lead them into a place more primitive than the tunnel, maybe a cave or even a sewer. Instead, they stood at the end of what looked like a hotel corridor, painted a calming green, with little brass fixtures high on the wall every twenty feet or so; fixtures that gave off an indirect illumination. The carpet was a deeper green, and, while a little worn here and there, showed no signs of dust or other debris.

Lenny stared down the hall. He and his team members had just come out of a sub-sub-basement. And the land around South Station was incredibly flat. So it wasn't as if they had walked to a hillside. Which led to yet another question: Who would build a hotel underground?

"Uh, guys—" Lenny began.

"Someone has been here recently," Lenore said.

"Could harbor ghosts," Karnowski agreed. "Perhaps we get information."

The Baron wrinkled his nose. "Someone has been here very recently. And he was eating onions."

"Lenny should lead way," Karnowski said.

"His abilities found a much more civilized walk for us. . . ." Lenore paused, before adding, "and one that seems relatively safe."

Still not one word about the underground hotel.

"But, guys—" Lenny began again.

"I sense problems with our team," the Baron interrupted with a frown. "Our whole approach is wrong. Why doesn't Ms. Siggenbottom ever pick the charismatic one to lead? The matinee idol looks, the well-tailored cape with the tasteful red lining, the attractive ring with the ancient family crest, it all eloquently says 'leader'! Let's look at the facts. A vampire's powers are well documented. Vampires are strong. Vampires are swift. Vampires are feared."

"Vampires talk too much," Lenore added.

"Vampires not know how to work with team," Karnowski pitched in.

Lenny knew what the Baron was talking about. Until S's pep talk, he had never felt like a leader type.

Lenore sighed. "It's different without Withers."

Karnowski nodded with a glance at Lenny. "Withers was front man."

The Baron sniffed. "Even I must admit that Withers had his uses."

"When people screamed 'Oh my god, what is that?' it gave us a moment to plan," Lenore added wistfully.

"Withers also very good at tunneling."

It was the Baron's turn to study Lenny. "And our newest member?"

"He got us here." Lenore arched her eyebrows at Lenny one more time. "It seems he'll be good at something. I'm just not quite sure what."

Lenny had had enough. "Guys!" he shouted. "Does everybody realize we're in a hotel—deep underground?"

The other three glanced at each other.

"It only proves my point," the Baron replied.

"What he lacks in experience," Lenore retorted, "he will make up in talent."

Karnowski looked straight at Lenny. "Is not strangest thing you will see today. Lead on."

Lenny didn't know what to say to that, so he kept on walking.

For what looked like a hotel corridor, Lenny did not see all that many doors. One would occasionally show up on one side or the other as they continued down the lengthy hall, each door made of highly polished, dark wood. None of the doors even had room numbers.

"I wonder if these are intended as deluxe accommodations," the vampire mused, "for my kind."

"It would certainly be a step up from the coffins," Lenore agreed.

Lenny had almost forgotten about the coffins—the four coffins—including the one that hadn't opened. That was something else he hadn't asked about—maybe because he didn't want to know.

"Real rooms? No doubt filled with native soil." Karnowski nodded. "Wives would like that."

The Baron turned even paler than usual. "Please. Let us not talk about my—wives."

"This door is—open." Lenore waved at a door that stood slightly ajar on one side of the hall.

The door swung inward—all by itself—to reveal total darkness, perfectly in keeping with a hotel built far underground, perfectly hiding whatever waited on the other side. Lenny felt more conflicted than usual.

"I wouldn't go in there," he said before he could think about it.

"Room is trap," Karnowski agreed, holding up a hand in warning. "Wait for it." He turned to the door. "Enough hiding! Come out this minute!"

A white translucent figure drifted up from the darkness.

"Ooooooooh?" A faint voice, little more than a mournful whisper, issued from between the spirit's broken teeth.

Karnowski's frown deepened. "Who are you? What is your purpose?"

"Whoooo's asking?" the spirit whispered.

"Karnowski, the Ghost Finder! And you have been found."

"I suppoooose I have." The ghost sounded as if it couldn't care less. It paused, then issued a mournful sigh. "I'm not scaring you at all, am I? So much for the wailing. You ghost finders don't buy that sort of thing." Two dark smudges where the eyes should be looked past Karnowski at the rest of his party. "But I see—others—across the hall. Don't you think they deserve a good scare?"

The ghost finder shook his head. "Forget about them. Why do you wait by this trap?"

"You think I have a choice?" The spirit looked wistfully at the others. "I wandered here, just like you. Just like the 147 other spirits who are trapped down here with me. But am I bitter? One day, I find myself in an underground hotel, of all things. I go exploring. What a great adventure! I open this door, fall to my death. Splat! Right down there on those sharpened stakes you so narrowly avoided. But do I regret my actions?"

"You know nothing about who made this trap?" Karnowski demanded.

The ghost sighed. "We all have our theories. All 148 of us. But who can even think straight with all that moaning and wailing all the time?. You think I don't want to know the why of all this?"

Lenore stepped up next to Karnowski. "Perhaps we might take a different approach. Do you remember what you were called in life?"

"Now everybody's asking me questions?" The spirit's dark smudges stared at the ghost finder. "Can't I just haunt one or two of you? Just for a minute? A little shrieking, some energetic chain rattling? You might even enjoy it!" The ghost glanced back at the door. "You do realize we take turns floating up from the pit. Do you know how long you have to wait to get past 147 others?"

Karnowski seemed unfazed by the spirit's pleas. "Answer young woman's question. What was your name in life?"

"Oh, that's"—the ghost paused, lost for an instant in spectral concentration—"not easy at all. Jeannie, somebody was called Jeannie. That could have been me. Or possibly Ernesto. Gustav was a name that was bandied about quite a bit. And then there was Lugnut . . ."

The Baron stepped forward to join the others. "We are wasting our time here. The spirit knows nothing."

"I probably know quite a lot, if only I could remember it," the ghost retorted. "All that shrieking and wailing down there can do a number on your concentration. But do I complain?"

"Enough with this dead end!" The vampire puffed up his tuxedoed chest. "It is time, at last, to demonstrate my powers!"

Both Karnowksi and Lenore frowned.

"Are you sure?" the ghost finder asked.

"Look at the time!" Lenore glanced impatiently at her wrist, even though she wasn't wearing a watch.

"This will take but a moment." The Baron's triumphant smile showed the tips of his fangs. "You are not the only one with resources. These dark places are full of creatures of the night. Come to me, my darlings!"

Lenny jumped. The hall carpet was moving. No, not the rug, but hundreds of creatures on the rug, creatures with brown fur and gray fur, even the occasional white fur.

"Rats?" the ghost cried. "How can I compete with rats?"

"My creatures!" the Baron called. The rodents chittered in reply, as they circled around the party, weaving back and forth so that they narrowly avoided overrunning Lenny's shoes.

"Now we will get the truth!" the vampire cried in triumph. "Tell me, my creatures! What is out goal?"

And the rats answered in a choral singsong:
Nice to see you honored master
This place you're in's one big disaster!
You'll have to outdo
The legions of Foo
If you want to get out there and ask her

The chant was high pitched, but perfectly understandable. Not only were the rats talking in unison, but also in some sort of verse. Lenny noticed something strangely familiar about that rhyme scheme.

"Then we know it's Foo," Karnowski said.

"And Foo knows we're here!" Lenore said with equal conviction.

Lenny didn't feel quite so enthusiastic. "Who's Foo? And what about the rest of it? 'If you want to ask her'? Who's her?"

The Baron shrugged. "Talking with my creatures is not an exact science."

"Hello! Lonely, wandering spirit still in the hallway!" the ghost interjected. "Who wants to listen to rats when you can talk about me?"

"If you had something useful to say . . ." Karnowski left the rest of the thought unsaid.

"Hey! You spend weeks wailing and months moaning, see if it

doesn't dampen your conversation."

Lenny had had enough of this. As unpleasant as the rats might be, at least they could provide some clues as to the group's destination. Lenny tugged on the Baron's cape.

"Can I ask a question?"

The vampire waved at the rats. "Whatever you want. My creatures are at your service. What do you need?"

Need? Lenny hadn't actually thought that far ahead. Perhaps he should ask the most important question of all.

He cleared his throat. "Please tell me—uh—creatures: What do I have to do with all of this?"

And the rats sang again:
There once was a young man named Lenny
Who came here with nary a penny
Before this has passed
He'll look back to his past
And find that his problems were many.

Lenny stared down at the mass of vermin. "That isn't helpful at all."

"I referred to them as informative," the Baron replied brusquely. "Never did I suggest they might actually be helpful."

Lenny shook his head in disbelief. "And—the rats speak in limericks?"

Lenore nodded. "The ways of the supernatural are beyond our understanding."

The Baron stepped forward. "I should lead the way now. Pits are not so deadly to those who can sprout wings."

Somebody else would lead the way? Really? Lenny remembered to breathe again. The four of them moved forward slowly, staying close together. The corridor ended up ahead. He half expected to see an elevator, but instead the hall reached a T-junction, with more hallway leading in either direction. They paused just before the junction.

As far as Lenny could tell, the two corridors looked exactly alike. Now would be a good time for whatever "talent" he had to speak up and tell them which way to go.

"Look!" Lenore pointed above another of those brass light fixtures. There, written in white chalk, were the words BAD GUYS THIS WAY! and an arrow pointing left.

Lenore frowned. "Either Lenny's powers manifest themselves in even more surprising ways—"

"—or we have guide," Karnowski finished her sentence.

"The man who has eaten onions," the Baron concluded.

Lenny realized his team had stopped walking.

"Perhaps he wishes to help us," Lenore suggested.

"Perhaps is trap," Karnowski countered.

"Vampires are not afraid of traps."

"That's good," Lenny replied with more conviction than he felt. He turned to the left. "Because this is the way we're going." It was only after he started walking that Lenny realized he was leading the group once more.

His foot hit something hard. Lenny yelped as he fell forward on the carpet.

"Wait!" Lenore announced with authority.

Nobody moved.

"Is another trap?"

The Baron let his hands turn to mist. "There is a pressure plate hidden beneath the carpet."

Lenore nodded. "If one of us stepped on it, it would have released dozens of knives, spring-loaded behind the walls to either side. Lucky for us, Lenny tripped over it instead."

"The plate is flush with the floor," the Baron said as his hands rematerialized before him. "How could anybody trip?"

"Luck has nothing to do with it," Lenore replied.

"Is Lenny," Karnowski agreed.

"Perhaps." The Baron still looked skeptical. "But what now?"

Lenny cautiously got to his feet on the far side of the trap. "We walk around it."

The others stepped carefully past the trap as they continued down the hall.

"No more ghosts," Karnowski commented as they walked. "At least, no new ghosts."

"No other threats that I can smell," the Baron added.

Lenore extended both her hands, palms outward, as though she was feeling the air. "The signs are becoming more uncertain. There is danger in the distance." She shook her head. "I know no more."

Karnowski nodded. "Hopefully is in distance we are not going."

Lenny frowned. Didn't evil traps come in threes? No, maybe that was plane crashes.

Lenore said nothing more. Lenny guessed that the main benefit of her gift was to give you time to worry.

They continued to walk until Lenny saw a wall ahead. At first he thought it would lead into another corridor, but as he got closer, it was looking more like a dead end. The hallway simply stopped.

High above them on this final wall was a red exit sign. Except this one was a bit bigger than usual, and in front of the red exit was another word: NO.

"What we do now?" Karnowski asked.

This time, Lenny saw it first.

That same chalked scrawl. Two words: press here. And next to the words, a larger chalk X.

Lenny pushed the chalk mark. The wall rolled away.

Lenore gasped.

"Karnowski has never!" the ghost finder exclaimed.

The Baron muttered something in Romanian under his breath.

Lenny had to agree. A hotel hallway he could accept. This was something else altogether.

Seven

Lenny felt like he had stepped into another world. He was surrounded by steel and chrome.

"Is airline terminal!" Karnowski said.

"Something like it," Lenore agreed. She nodded toward a moving walkway a few feet in front of them. "It's certainly designed to get people from here to there."

"I've flown around the world at night." The Baron's cape fluttered in an air-conditioned breeze as he gazed up at the high, vaulted ceiling. "Even my centuries of experience have seen nothing like this!"

The team had walked forward as they stared in wonder at their surroundings. Lenny now stood before the walkway, a great, moving metal belt, maybe six feet across with waist-high walls to either side. The machine hummed as it moved, the moving metal stretching out before them into the distance.

"Shall we?" Lenny asked.

Lenore raised a single, gloved hand to point ahead. "The other who precedes us has already passed this way."

"But he gains distance," the Baron added. "The onions are receding."

"This is middle of huge expanse," Karnowski whispered. "Ghosts huddle nearby." His frown deepened. "We are being followed."

"Many things lurk nearby," Lenore agreed, "and many of them are not friendly."

"I detect many creatures in the distance. And beyond the smell of onions, I detect the odor of death." The Baron's cape billowed dramatically.

Lenny's three teammates looked at each other. All three of them smiled. Lenny turned to the rather more expansive vista before them, much too nice now to be called a tunnel. This was more a modern, brightly lit corridor.

The moving walkway propelled them through the huge room, full of modular furniture, all of it unoccupied. Then the walls of the first great expanse closed in on either side, until they traveled through a new tunnel. It was almost the total opposite of the tunnel they had taken before.

Spotlights lined the ceiling above them so that the walls to either side were too brightly lit. The lights pointed to a seemingly endless row of colorful posters plastered to the walls that they passed, posters of figures in flowing red robes and hoods. Some of the figures were waving, others seemed to be jumping or running. There were even a couple seated in overstuffed chairs. But the red robes were only a secondary part of each poster, for each sheet was dominated by a brightly colored slogan; big letters in vibrant yellow, blue, or green.

He read the slogans one after another as the walkway quietly moved them past.

It's good to be evil!
Everything will be nifty when we rule the world.
Foo is with you! (This one was all type, with no hooded figure at all.)
Nothing says lovin' like world domination in the oven!

"Are deep in enemy territory." Karnowski's voice was hushed.

Lenore nodded. "This has gone much farther than any of us thought."

Even the Baron seemed impressed. "How have they managed to build something like this?"

Corruption pays! another poster answered his question. The slogans kept on coming:

Happy under the hood! Follow the plan! A couple of *Foo is with you!* one right after another.

"Look!" Lenore pointed at a poster up ahead. It showed a hooded figure on a cell phone, the large image partially obscured by a large black X. But it was the slogan that made the breath catch in Lenny's throat.

Loose lips alert lenny!

Everyone stared as the slogan passed by.

"Is spy in Terrifitemps!" Karnowski whispered.

"Not surprising," Lenore replied. "We are no more secret than those mysterious groups we fight."

It might be stranger than any of his team realized. Lenny decided it was time to tell them about his own personal mysterious stranger.

"Um, guys? We may have a spy on our side." He quickly described his encounter with the man in the dirty jumpsuit.

"You mean," Lenore said as she pointed ahead, "someone who looks like that?"

Lenny looked ahead to see a white, jumpsuited leg disappear though a door.

"Is your S, yes?" Karnowski asked.

The Baron shook his cape in agitation. "So Lenny is getting outside help? I suspected as much all along!"

"Mysterious stranger not negate Lenny's power!" Karnowski insisted. "Who says S appears without Lenny?"

Lenore turned to Lenny and smiled. "The ways of Terrifitemps are deep and mysterious."

Lenny's phone rang again.

"You have a phone?" the Baron said in surprise.

"You can get a call down here?" Lenore echoed in much the same tone.

"Enemy lair has Wi-Fi," Karnowski replied knowingly.

Lenny didn't think this was a good time to answer the phone. They had reached the end of the moving walkway, as they were deposited, one by one, on a carpeted hall that led to three rooms. It was time to make a decision.

"One of doors leads to goal," Karnowski said before Lenny could even think about it.

"But which one?" Lenore asked. "And what about the other two?" She frowned at the leftmost door. "A lady has passed here recently."

The Baron nodded at the door on the far right. "The room beyond that one smells of tiger."

Lenny knew the decision was his even before the others looked at him. Besides, he was pretty sure he'd seen S disappear through the door in the middle.

"We go this way," he said as he stepped forward and turned the knob. The door swung open to reveal a lightless space beyond.

No second thoughts. If Lenny was to fulfill Ms. Siggenbottom's faith in him, he had to act. He stepped forward, and the others followed.

The door swung shut behind them with an all-too-loud thump and an almost-as-loud click. A single bright light switched on overhead to illuminate the far wall, which was completely covered by a huge, moving image of the robed Foo.

"Ha ha ha ha ha!" echoed from somewhere above. "Ha ha ha ha ha!"

"Is evil laughter!" Karnowski shouted.

"Foo has lured us into his trap!"

Lenore ignored the laughter and walked to her left to get a closer look at the nearest wall. Lenny glanced back at the painting. Foo's giant eyes were moving, the pupils following Lenore as she ran her hand along the wall's smooth surface.

"Ha ha ha ha!" the annoying, echoing laughter continued. "And did I mention, ha!"

Karnowski pounded at the poster. The Baron studied the ceiling overhead. The increasingly tedious laughter started again.

"Cannot happen!" Karnowski cried in frustration. "We are Terrifitemps!"

"Wait a minute!" Lenny called. "So they've got us trapped here for a minute! We've found ways around all our earlier obstacles!"

"Look!" Lenore called, pointing at the floor. Water was rising through the carpet to soak their shoes. The laughter redoubled as the large eyes in the painting looked from one of their team to the next, seemingly gloating at his triumph.

Lenny was getting more peeved by the minute. "So we're trapped here for a minute and the room is filling with water! I'm sure all of you have faced far worse obstacles in the past."

The Baron held up his hand in warning. "Do I smell—gas?"

"Ha ha ha ha ha!" the laughter came even louder, thundering over the sound of rushing water and hissing gas.

"Wait a minute!" Lenny shouted. "So we're temporarily trapped in a room filling with water in which a deadly—" He stopped himself. Actually, it did sound pretty desperate. And the more he shouted at the others, the more the evil genius threw at them. Maybe he should stop before the bad guy released the poisonous water snakes or something.

He looked up at Foo's gloating eyeballs. Boy, would he like to poke the laughter right out of those.

"Ha ha ha!" Foo began again.

Well, why not? Lenny took a running leap across the room.

"Ha ha ha ha," Foo continued. "Ha ha—oh, nuts!" as Lenny slapped at his target with the heel of his hand.

The eyes disappeared from the huge portrait, and the wall lifted out of sight.

Lenny led the others forward at a run before the wall could lower again. They found themselves in yet another room, this one filled with video screens, each showing a different view of the room, so that they could watch themselves walking from a dozen different angles as they turned from one screen to another.

The screens lined the walls on three sides before them. Once again, Lenny could see no clear exit. He walked toward a screen on the far side of the room, his image steadily growing larger from the video feed placed directly above the screen. Every screen had a single red button beneath it. Lenny chose to press the one in front of him.

All the screens went blank for an instant, then flared back to life. They now showed the exact same picture—some sort of control room, filled with busy figures in lab coats and large machines with lots of flashing lights. At the very center of each screen were two figures—one a short, balding man with a worried expression who kept glancing at the other figure, who was tall and wearing a hood and robe of jet black.

The man in black waved his robes in an agitated fashion. "How could this possibly happen?"

The shorter fellow cringed as he spoke. "Beg pardon, Your Evilness?"

"Three times they have almost fallen into our trap! Almost fallen, almost crushed, almost drowned, but at the last minute, they save themselves!"

The shorter man nodded so rapidly, Lenny half expected his head to bounce free of his body. "Truly unthinkable, Your Awfulness."

"Our plan is so simple!" The tall figure seemed to relax a bit as he thought of it. "We have already neutralized their leader. Now, once we destroy their elite team, they will be completely demoralized." He chuckled the slightest bit. "Yet we cannot administer the fatal blow. The fools seem to sense our intentions! How is this possible?"

The short man grew even paler than before. "Oh dear, Your Vileness. I was hoping I could correct it before you noticed—"

But the man-in-black's robes were fluttering once more. "What happened to our video feed? Why can't I see them on our screens? Why is the red light flashing over 'send'?"

"You are truly the master of evil!" The bald fellow talked so fast, Lenny had trouble making out distinct words. "What has happened is unthinkable!"

The figure in black stared straight ahead, his voice ominously devoid of emotion. "My relay reversed the video feed. Instead of watching them, they are watching us."

"I will correct it immediately, O Mighty One. We will take steps to make sure it never happens—" His hurried words turned into a scream as the hooded one pulled a lever at his side and the bald man dropped from sight.

"At least the crocodiles in the pit below have had a bit to eat." The man in black was silent for a moment. He turned to the back of his room. "I have only begun to plot. I need another minion—now!"

The screen went blank.

"Is Foo!" Karnowski whispered, as the video screen before them rolled away to reveal a larger space beyond.

"Look!" Lenore called, as all four of them noticed the silver escalator, going up.

Lenny's phone rang one more time.

Eight

Lenny looked at his phone. Sheila had left him a text message. *trouble. need ur help.*

"Karnowski not use phone," the tall man said from his position next down on the escalator. "Gives static to ghosts."

"Modern technology often interferes with our powers," Lenore agreed. "So we've learned to stay away from it."

"I would get calls from wives," the Baron added morosely.

"But Lenny is different," Lenore continued. "He'll bring Terrifitemps into the twenty-first century!"

At the moment, Lenny was mostly worrying about the text message. Trouble? That could mean anything.

where r u? he texted back.

The escalator took them up, and then it took them up some more. Wherever they had ended up, somewhere around South Station, or somewhere in South Boston, or somewhere on Mars, they had been deep, deep below the ground.

grabbed by foo! Sheila texted back. *he wants*

And then nothing. Lenny stared at the phone.

"Something has gone wrong," Lenore said.

"I had a visitor this morning," Lenny replied. "Someone I haven't seen in years. And now—Foo's got her!"

The Baron looked toward the ceiling. "The master of evil must be watching our every move!"

"Is top of escalator!" Karnowski called. "Now we see action!"

Lenny realized he was ready. First his stamp collection, and now Sheila. He was in the middle of this whether he wanted to be or not.

"Well," Lenore added, "perhaps action isn't the best description."

And indeed, the escalator deposited them onto a tidy brick floor, in a tidy but small brick room, with a narrow—yet tidy—brick staircase before them. Except the staircase seemed to lead only to an equally tidy brick ceiling. Lenny took a quick walk around the room and saw that the walls were not quite so clean as they had first appeared, as the bricks were covered here and there by faint chalk markings. *Foo and you!* was written in yellow; *Phoo rules!* in white; *Pffffoooo!* showed up in bright pink; *Many men smoke but foo—* (the rest was too smeared to read). And finally, written in a bilious green: *Ffw! Ffw! Ffw!*

"F-f-w?" Lenny asked.

"Is Foo in Welsh," Karnowski replied.

Lenny stared at the strange graffiti. If nothing else, these Foo folk were enthusiastic.

"And now?" the Baron said with menacing intent.

Everybody looked at Lenny. He shrugged and walked to the staircase, then climbed the first three steps. Nothing changed.

What now? Lenny found himself getting the slightest bit annoyed. This so-called ability of his had left him feeling helpless again. He stomped backward down the steps. Everybody was still looking at him. What did they expect?

"Wait!" Karnowski said.

With a quiet grinding of gears, a panel in the ceiling—painted to match the surrounding bricks—slid away.

At least nobody mentioned Ms. Siggenbottom this time around. The Baron stepped forward. "One who knows how to deal with danger should lead the way."

Lenny wasn't going to argue. Just because things happened around him didn't mean they would be good things. He let the others go before him and then he, too, climbed the stairs.

He climbed out under bright starlight into what he first thought was an open field. Then he realized the ground was hard beneath his feet—hard and dark. The field was paved. He heard a faint whirring noise as the hatchway closed behind him. From above, the closed hatchway looked like a manhole cover, with the words city of boston stamped on its dull-gray surface.

Lenore turned back to look at him. "You've led us here?"

"Leading Karnowski to answers," Karnowski added as he, too, stepped back toward Lenny. The tall man raised a cautionary hand. "Now Karnowski senses ghosts."

The Baron seemed to float more than walk as he silently joined the others on the asphalt plain. "We are not alone," the Baron added. "There are others all around us."

"We have left the safety of the tunnels behind," Lenore agreed. "We have walked into danger."

Karnowski added, "Now let fun begin."

Once again, Lenny's companions were all smiles. He realized the other three were really enjoying themselves.

"Where is here?" Lenny asked as his eyes adjusted to his starlit surroundings. The pavement went on for some distance in all directions, descending into a gully a few hundred feet to his left. A few hundred feet in the other direction, the asphalt was interrupted by great cement pilings that supported an overhead road. Despite the warnings of his team, Lenny could see no other signs of life.

Karnowski surveyed their grim surroundings. "Once this was a thriving community, full of warehouses and distribution centers."

Lenny turned around, marveling that this place had ever been full of life. The expanse was silent, save for the occasional quiet rumble of a truck on the distant highway. He felt as if the city he knew had disappeared. What disaster could have caused this?

"Urban renewal," Lenore replied, as if she could again read his thoughts. "As Karnowski said, this space once held row upon row of warehouses, small businesses, the all-important sandwich shops. Now, a vast and empty parking lot."

She pointed past Lenny to a spot high overhead. He turned to see a large sign looming out of the gloom: ALL-DAY PARKING $13.

He looked beyond the sign and saw that the asphalt did not actually go on forever. A few hundred feet away the dark ground gave way to a strip of lighter gray. A sidewalk, with another one on the other side of a darker street. In the distance he saw a row of streetlights, only half of which were working. The manhole cover was correct—they were still in some part of Boston, but in the middle of blocks and blocks of nothing. He turned back to the pillars supporting the road overhead. Far beyond them, Lenny thought he could see the lights of a tall building or two—office buildings?

The Baron stepped in front of Lenny, his cape unfurling behind him despite the lack of a breeze. He pointed into the distance. "My superior vampire senses detect our destination."

He walked forward, beckoning for the others to join him. They followed slowly, being careful not to trip over any of the large cracks and holes in the asphalt.

"There!" the vampire announced. Lenny peered ahead and saw a dim light in the shadowy area beneath the highway. They walked closer, until he saw what appeared to be brown canvas walls, barely illuminated by a pair of small lanterns—like a display you'd find at a camping store. Someone had erected tents in the space beneath the highway.

Karnowski raised a hand in warning, pointing to the left of the canvas walls. Deeper in that shadowed space was a group of figures, all wearing blood-red, hooded robes.

Lenny could hear something, too, in the silences between the rumble of trucks above; a faint, sonorous chanting, rising and falling, repeating the same phrase over and over.

"Hummina hummina hummina . . ."

"What does that mean?" Lenny asked. "Who are they?"

"Know from hidden tunnels, not to mention flashy posters! They are minions of Foo!"

Lenny tried to fit this new image with their experience in the tunnels. "But why—if they control hotels filled with dangerous traps and subterranean transportation stations plastered with propaganda posters—why are they hiding in tents?"

"Camouflage," Lenore explained. "Secret societies like to appear as less than they actually are."

"They can hide even from my kind," the Baron agreed.

"Even now, we may be dealing with more than a single group of minions. It's so difficult to tell," Lenore replied with a frown. "The mysterious hood has never been out of fashion." She glanced at Karnowski. "So far, we've only talked to Lenny about the secret societies. What if Foo is controlling one of the really secret secret societies?"

Karnowski nodded. "What we know of these shadow associations? Rumors, innuendoes, names half heard above roar of moving train, words half uttered before messenger suddenly shot."

Messenger shot? Lenny thought. Those things didn't really—

He reminded himself he was watching a group of weirdly chanting figures in blood-red robes.

"But we have ways to fight them, don't we?"

"Ghosts, supernatural strength, certain psychic abilities, or so I've heard," the Baron agreed. "And, until recently, the element of surprise the werevole brings. We do not yet know how you will replace that."

"Here is different," Karnowski replied. "Have supernatural strength—banished all ghosts from the vicinity." The tall man gasped, his pale face drained of whatever blood remained. "Karnowski stand corrected. They have banished all ghosts but—one." For the first time since Lenny had met the man, Karnowski looked genuinely shaken.

"Oh no," Lenore agreed. The last two words were barely a whisper.

"Are we in danger?" Lenny whispered back.

"Not danger," Karnowski replied. "Just Bob."

"Bob the horse?" the Baron managed to hiss despite his fangs.

"What other Bob is there?" Lenore pointed into the middle distance, somewhere to the left of the chanting figures. Something semitransparent, and blue, galloped toward them across the vast parking lot. It was shaped like a horse, it moved like a horse, it looked like a horse in every way but one (well, except for the fact that the horse was blue). This was the first time Lenny had ever seen a horse who was smiling.

"Wow, guys!" The horse spoke in a deep but cheerful voice. "You're really in trouble this time!"

"Nice to see you, too, Bob," Lenore replied in a clipped tone that implied anything but "nice." "Everything is under control."

Bob pranced eagerly before them. "Of course it is! I'm sure you've figured some way out of the certain death creeping up on you this very minute!" He glanced at the red hoods, then turned his snout out toward the darkness of the fields, as though waiting for some invisible menace. "You know, nobody's ever faced them and lived! I'm just sayin.'" Bob glanced at Lenny. "Hey! How come no one introduced me to the new guy?"

"I'm Lenny." He started to raise his right arm. But how do you shake hands with a horse—especially a ghost horse? "And you're Bob?" he said instead.

"Right the first time. And you can see me, too?" Bob did a little happy canter. "Ms. S. sure knows how to pick them!"

"He's talking, isn't he?" the Baron said in a hushed voice. "What if someone among the enemy can hear ghosts?"

"Karnowski can see ghosts clearly," Lenore explained. "I sense them more than see them, and I can hear them after a fashion if I really concentrate, but only like a faint voice on the radio. The Baron, unfortunately, can barely hear or see those on the spectral plane."

"I have trained myself for Terrifitemps!" The Baron squinted in Bob's general direction. "Although I sometimes wonder why I bother."

"Who makes up these rules, anyways?" Bob chimed in. "None of those guys in red care about me. I'm just a pooka! It would be different if I could die a horrible death at their deranged bidding!"

"Is good, Bob," Karnowski interjected. "But could you give little peace and quiet? Karnowski need to concentrate."

The ghost horse shook his head agreeably. "Hey, anybody else would have run! But here you are talkin.' How brave is that? Sure, go ahead and stick around, even though it's like signing your death warrant. But do you guys care?"

Lenore glanced at Lenny, a hint of despair in her eyes. "Could you talk to Bob"—she waved back the way they had come—"somewhere over there?"

"Sure!" Lenny waved the horse to follow him as the three other team members gathered together to talk. Maybe he could get some useful information from this apparition. "So. You really know your way around here, huh?"

"Nothing a skilled pooka can't handle!" Bob agreed.

Lenny frowned. This was even further beyond his understanding than usual.

"What do you do as a pooka?"

Bob paused for an instant before he answered. "Mostly, we pook."

That didn't tell Lenny anything. He tried again. "How do you pook?"

"You'd know if you were a pooka," Bob replied with a toss of its ghostly mane. "How'd you get this job, anyway?"

Lenny still wasn't quite sure about that himself. "It's a long story."

"Isn't it always," Bob said with a sigh. "You know, I've wanted to work at Terrifitemps for a long time. Such brave, foolhardy people. I'd fit right in. Someday, they'll see how valuable a pooka can be." He glanced back at the gathering in the underpass. "The vengeful horde should be noticing you just about now. Pookas know that sort of thing."

Lenny saw movement among the robes. The group was standing now. Some of them pointed and waved their hands. But none of them made any move to come any closer.

"Uh-oh," Bob said. "Now that's really bad."

Lenore ran toward them. "We're splitting into two teams!" she said hurriedly. "The Baron can turn insubstantial, and get close to them, hopefully without their notice. Karnowski has overcome our enemy's primitive wards and is even now calling up his legions of ghosts, who can move among the hooded ones and disrupt whatever they plan to do."

That meant Lenny and Lenore were the other team. He was surprised how happy that made him. "And what should we do?"

"We," Lenore said as she grabbed his elbow, "are taking the bus."

"There's a bus?" Lenny asked.

Lenore waved at the vast expanse around them. "How else can people get to their cars?"

"It's been nice, guys!" Bob called over his shoulder as he galloped away. "But I think it's time for even me to leave."

A great wailing rose from the hooded crowd. The asphalt in front of them began to glow a dull blue.

"We need to get out of here!" Lenore shouted. "Now."

Lenny saw small, blue flames erupt from the pavement closest to the hooded crowd, then spread across the glowing surface, rushing toward them.

Lenny turned and ran. That bus was sounding better and better.

He stumbled when his feet hit the sidewalk. He ran into the street, then leaped onto the sidewalk on the other side, not really knowing what he was running toward, only trying to escape that ever-warmer blue light behind him.

His legs felt like lead. His lungs like they would burst. But still he ran. A wind sprang up. It felt cool against his skin.

Lenny stopped. He was surrounded by darkness. The blue glowing flames were gone.

He looked around. The highway was still on his left, maybe farther away than before. He saw no sign of Lenore, or any of the others. He was alone, with no idea where he was or where he was going.

"Woo-hoo!" a voice said in his ear. "I always like a little scare!"

He turned to see a smiling Bob the horse.

"Where is everybody?" Lenny asked.

"Your friends from Terrifitemps?" Bob replied with a cheerful whinny. "Probably standing together in one final, futile attempt to turn back the tide of total destruction." The pooka sadly shook its blue mane. "I wish you had their chance of survival."

A chorus of voices roared behind them. Lenny spun toward the noise and saw a dozen figures in red robes running toward them.

A dozen to one? Lenny thought. Every one of the figures rushing in their direction was brandishing some sort of sharp object.

His luck—or his ability—or whatever they had called it—had finally run out on him.

The first of the red hoods ran at him with a sword. Its eyes were wild behind the hood. "Infidel!" it screamed. Lenny stumbled backward, losing his balance. He sat down heavily on the pavement as the sword whistled overhead.

The second robe charged right behind the first, swinging what looked like a medieval mace. "Assassin!"

The new attacker lost its footing as Bob the horse reared before it.

"Don't thank me yet!" Bob called over his shoulder. "I'm only delaying the inevitable!"

A third robed figure attacked with what looked like an ancient ceremonial dagger. This close the eyes that showed behind his mask seemed to have no pupils.

"Stamp collector!" it screamed. The dagger whipped toward Lenny's chest and would have hit him if the previous two robed figures had not regained their balance and decided to renew their attack at the same instant. Sword clashed with mace. Dagger bounced off sword. Flowing red robes tangled together, so Lenny could no longer tell where one assailant ended and the next began. The three fell to the pavement as a heaving, thrashing mass.

"Boy," Bob called from beyond the entangled enemies. "Your luck just keeps getting worse!"

"What?" Lenny demanded. What was the pooka talking about this time?

"Only something worse than death itself!" Bob replied.

It was then that the world went dark.

Nine

"Okay, I'm ready!" a new voice called close to Lenny's right side. "Where's that ghost-finder guy?"

Lenny stared at the new arrival. Someone, or something, stood before him, somehow dispersing the unnatural gloom with an equally unnatural radiance. The glowing white figure was even more insubstantial than Bob, yet there was something vaguely familiar about the newcomer.

The ghost finder? Lenny thought. "Karnowski? We were separated. I have no idea where he is." Lenny stared off into the gloom. "I have no idea where we are."

"I'd say," Bob added, "that we were in trouble."

Lenny turned to the pooka and saw half a dozen figures silhouetted by streetlights rushing in their direction. Most of the hooded figures brandished knives, which, with their oddly curved blades, might be ceremonial, though their edges still looked plenty sharp. The ones without knives simply brandished guns.

"Oh," Lenny said. In the confusion, he had forgotten to flee.

"Excuse me," the spectral stranger remarked as he turned toward the onrushing mob. Its ghostly image grew tenfold, sprouting half a dozen arms, all of which held sharp claws. It reared up before the approaching crowd.

The running horde slowed, then staggered to a halt.

"Rarrarrarrharrarr!" the specter roared.

The hooded figures ran in terror.

The ghost returned to its earlier indistinct form.

"Couldn't they see we were talking? Now where were we? We've met before, back in the hotel. I'm—" The ghost sighed. "Not remembering your name makes it very difficult to introduce yourself."

Now Lenny recalled the ghost. "You were the fellow from the pit? I thought you were trapped there."

"So did I. Apparently I just had nowhere to go. But then Karnowski called. Here I am, out and about, ready to see the sights." The ghost paused. "There's not much to look at around here."

"It's the problem with dark places," Bob agreed. "Too much dark."

"I don't care," the spirit replied. "I've come to join a team of bold adventurers. You will lead me to confront danger and perform noble deeds! Tell me, adventurers, where are you bound?"

"Um," Lenny answered, "I think we're trying to find a bus stop."

"Really?" The ghost paused again. "Well, I'm sure it must be a noble bus stop."

"I hate to interrupt," Bob interrupted, "but we're in even more trouble than we were before."

Lenny saw a couple of vague shapes approaching them through the gloom. Why was it that Bob only warned him about danger when it was too late to do anything about it?

The two figures drew closer, yet remained in shadow. At least Lenny could tell there were two of them. Where Bob was bright blue, and the ghost was a hazy white, the two newcomers wore dark raincoats, with the spaces above their collars still lost behind those persistent shadows. Lenny recognized them nonetheless. They, or another pair equally indistinct, had come calling on him at his apartment just before Sheila and the first day cover had disappeared. And they brought the darkness with them.

"Trouble again, huh?" the friendly ghost asked. "Time for me to go into action."

The specter once again grew in size. Lenny almost jumped. From this angle, Lenny could view the whole spirit, including its six eyes and the glow-in-the-dark teeth.

The shadowy figures watched the spirit grow.

Sparks flew as the ghost brandished its many claws. This was certainly holding Lenny's attention. The spirit was really getting into it.

The shadowy figures glanced at each other. The ghost opened its frightening jaw mere inches above them.

"Rohahahaharrrr!"

Lenny had trouble standing as the piercing cry washed over him.

The apparition returned to its original form with a satisfied chuckle. "Nothing like a good scare."

The all-too-shadowy fellows were still there.

"Very enthusiastic," one of them said.

"Still, it lacks a certain polish," the other replied. "We are here to collect Lenny Hodge. Is that one of you?"

"He has made friends with ghosts. That would fit with his profile."

"He may have escaped us before, but not again. We're almost entirely certain that he is the Lenny we are looking for."

"Without a shadow of a doubt. Well, perhaps a very small shadow. And why wouldn't he come with us? He will barely be inconvenienced at all. We simply need to ask him a few questions, run a few tests."

"Hardly any trouble at all. Unless we can't determine his special gift."

"That?" A hint of disappointment seemed to enter his cheery tone. "We might—only as a last resort—have to dissect him. Purely in the interests of science. How do humans deal with dissection?"

"I believe it tends to kill them."

"That would be unfortunate. Necessary, but unfortunate." His tone was resigned, and final.

The two shadow figures shifted slightly, so that they might actually be looking at Lenny. "But enough idle chitchat. You slipped through our fingers before."

"You are necessary to the completion. We must take you now."

Lenny wished he knew where the rest of his team had gone. They would be able to deal with this. But shouldn't his special gift be showing up? According to Ms. Siggenbottom, something should be happening right about now. An earthquake, maybe? A tornado? A meteor?

"But—" Lenny began. He couldn't think of anything to follow that.

Slowly, the two raincoats approached him.

"Hi guys." A cheerful voice popped up behind him. "What's up?"

The two newcomers stopped. They turned their shadowed faces to look at each other. Both turned back to Lenny.

"Is that Bob the horse?" two voices asked as one.

Lenny heard a quaver in their speech, a sound he hadn't heard before. He glanced over his shoulder. "You're back?"

Lenny hadn't even realized the horse was gone.

"Just taking care of pooka business!" Bob replied.

Lenny glanced back at the strangers. Instead of moving forward, the mysterious duo were ever so slowly moving away.

"We are almost certain we have an appointment elsewhere," one of them said.

"And there's always the chance—ever so slight—that we might be mistaken," the other added.

The two raincoats became one with the gloom.

Lenny looked out into the void where the two shadowy figures had stood. Bob the horse cantered up beside him.

"Nice fellows. Good listeners, too, if you can corner them. I remember one time—we must have talked for hours!" Bob whinnied with delight.

"They weren't even scared!" the ghost said by his other side. "What should I expect? Being stuck in that pit year after year, it dulls your edge." The ghost sighed, the sound of a chill wind in February. "Shouldn't we proceed with our quest?"

"Quest?" Lenny asked. Oh. The bus stop. Lenny not only had to learn to lead, he had to do it when other things got in the way.

Lenny saw a pool of light maybe a hundred feet away, with a small, half-enclosed structure and a black-and-red sign at the street corner.

"This way," he called to the others as he walked toward the light. Maybe he could have some time to think on the bus.

"Whoops!" said Bob the horse as they reached the bus stop. "Now this is really bad!"

The shelter was occupied—by a man wearing robes of royal purple. Robes, but no hood. He grinned as Lenny approached.

"We have not met, but I know you. You may call me Foo."

Well, Lenny thought, he was waiting for something to happen.

Ten

Lenny's two companions didn't seem particularly happy to see the newcomer.

"This is the man who made me what I am today!" the ghost complained.

"I doubt very much he could even pass the pooka test," Bob added.

Neither of these remarks made Lenny feel any better about his situation. He studied the man called Foo. For a mysterious cult leader, he looked awfully ordinary. Foo had a pasty complexion and thinning hair, and sported a smile that was as large as it was insincere. He looked like somebody's uncle who really should stop smoking. Especially if that uncle sold used cars.

Lenny looked to either side of the bus shelter and out into the street. The night was still and empty. Apparently Foo had come alone.

The cultist was still grinning. "You will want to come with us. Someone you know is waiting for your help." He held out a cell phone displaying a photo. Lenny looked at the screen. It revealed his ex-girlfriend, Sheila, tied to a chair. She had a gag in her mouth, but her eyes looked angry. Not scared. Sheila was never scared. But, as Lenny recalled, she could get angry.

"You don't want to disappoint her now," Foo added.

Lenny stared at the image. He thought of Sheila's disappearance, and the incomplete text message she had sent. How could he have known? Sheila leaving without another word? Sending messages he didn't understand? It was no different than the last few months of their relationship.

"This is exactly the sort of thing that turns people into ghosts," the nameless spirit remarked.

"But not into pookas!" Bob added enthusiastically. "That takes years of training!"

"You are not alone, are you?" Foo asked, smile still firmly in place. "Ghosts, perhaps? I can sense these things, although I cannot see them—yet."

So the overlord couldn't see Lenny's companions? Maybe Lenny could use that to his advantage. Still, how useful an insecure ghost and a pooka named Bob the horse would be was currently beyond him.

"I have people for that sort of thing," Foo continued. "Spectral resources. All a part of my management strategy."

"Management strategy," Lenny replied when it became apparent he should say something.

"The first phase of my team-building prognoses," Foo agreed. "Yes, my team. I hope, soon, to add you to their ranks." Foo's grin had grown larger. "The day you appeared on my radar, Mr. Hodge, is the day your life changed forever. My conquests are legion. My logistics are unsurpassed. Foo will soon control all media!" He looked past Lenny. "But I get ahead of myself. Our bus has arrived."

A large, black bus with tinted windows pulled up beside them. Air hissed as the door opened.

Lenny hesitated. This had to be a trap of some sort. But why were they letting him just climb onto the bus, rather than grabbing him, maybe sticking a bag over his head—all that kind of stuff?

He glanced at Foo. "Weren't you just trying to kill me?"

"Our strategy might have been a bit shortsighted. I assure you, Mr. Hodge, we have revised our projections. Just say I'm big enough to change my mind. Now, after you?" Foo waved the cell phone in Lenny's face. "Don't forget. You're on a mission."

Lenny glanced once more at the photo of his ex. Even though Sheila had dumped him, he had been surprised to realize he still had feelings for her. If he could do anything to help her, he would. Even if it meant going willingly with the legions of Foo.

Lenny climbed onto the bus.

"Don't worry, boss," a cheerful voice spoke right behind him. "Bob is with you every step of the way."

"Don't forget me!" a somewhat more uncertain voice added. "We will haunt another day. Do you think any of these folks scare easily?"

The bus door hissed closed behind them. It took Lenny a moment for his eyes to adjust to the indirect lighting. Foo guided him through a doorway just past the driver's seat.

Lenny stepped into a spacious lounge decorated with black couches, black tables, black curtains, and black throw pillows. Two people waited on the far couch.

"Wow!" the ghost said behind him. "After a few decades in a pit, this is what I call living!"

"May I introduce the rest of our company," Foo said as he stepped next to Lenny. He waved to the man on the left, a slight figure wearing a turban. "Swami Phillip Bruce Flalgalfaltal; one of the great mystics of a long European tradition."

"From the Bavarian Flalgalfaltals?" Bob whispered close by. "Wow, Lenny! You really rate!" The pooka and the ghost floated to Lenny's other side.

The man with the turban stood and bowed. "You may call me Swami Phil." He held up his hand. The gesture reminded Lenny of Lenore. "I sense the presence of others."

"See?" Foo was proud of himself. "Tell us more, Swami!"

The turbaned gentleman stared at the ceiling. "There are two spirits from the beyond." He waved dismissively. "The ghost is easily banished."

The air around the nameless spirit shimmered.

"What?" The ghost's image blurred, his voice fainter with every word. "But I just got out of that pit. This is no fair at all! You haven't heard the last . . ."

The spirit faded from sight.

"Excellent!" Foo cheered.

"The other one—might take a minute." The swami sighed. "It's a pooka."

Foo frowned at that. "A pooka? What does a pooka do?"

"Well, mostly they poo—" Swami Phil caught himself. "Explanations are useless. You would have to be an advanced swami to understand." He frowned in concentration. "I can at least banish him for a while. But pookas have a way of coming back!"

"Nothing will stand in the way of my five-year projections. Remove the pooka!" Foo commanded.

Swami Phil began an elaborate series of hand gestures—waves, slaps, finger wriggles, even a gesture that might be considered obscene in certain parts of Europe.

"Hah!" Bob the horse said. "An amateur!" He sidled up next to Lenny. "Don't worry, Boss! I'm here for the duration."

The swami began to shuffle and stomp his feet.

"You know, that's kind of catchy." Bob started to shuffle along.

Swami Phil redoubled his shuffle, clapping along to the beat. He began to hum.

"Now you're talking!" Bob began to dance. Lenny thought he was pretty good for someone with four hooved feet.

"One, two, cha-cha-cha!" Bob called.

The swami's hum grew louder. The melody surrounded them. Lenny could faintly hear a full orchestra playing along.

"Everybody mambo!" the pooka called. Bob danced through the wall of the bus, disappearing from sight.

"All clear," Swami Phil said as he sank back onto the couch. He was breathing heavily. Sweat darkened the base of his turban and rolled down his face.

"Excellent!" Foo replied. He glanced at the other, much larger occupant of the couch. "In all the excitement, I didn't introduce the other member of our team. This is Bruno."

Bruno took up fully two-thirds of the couch. He glared up at Lenny.

"He's paid mostly to be a silent menace," Foo added.

Lenny heard the bus's air brakes groan as the vehicle stopped abruptly, almost jarring him off his feet.

"But we've arrived!" Foo slapped him on the back. "It's time for you to rescue the fair maiden!"

Lenny had never thought of Sheila in quite that way before. But then, he'd never been on a rescue mission before, either.

"What do I need to do?"

"I think we should let Sheila decide that," Foo replied.

This was making an odd rescue even odder. Unless, of course, it was a trap. Which it probably was. Lenny wished the rest of his team was around to explain things.

Foo grabbed Lenny's arm and propelled him toward the front of the bus. Lenny glanced back to see Swami Phil and Bruno follow. Phil's first few steps were tentative, as if he hadn't regained the energy he'd used on his banishment spells. Bruno lumbered at the rear, making hardly any noise at all.

The bus doors hissed open, and Foo pushed Lenny forward. Lenny stepped out of the bus to find they were in a large parking garage. It seemed every bit as anonymous as that strange hotel hallway, or the huge urban wasteland where Foo's minions had pitched their tents. Lenny couldn't see any signs or markings identifying the place, besides the pillar opposite the door that informed them the bus was parked at G68. Foo led him through the parking lot and through a pair of unmarked doors.

Then Foo directed Lenny down an equally anonymous hallway, the sort you'd walk down to the men's room in a shopping mall. Dull yellow paint flaked from the walls. The group moved past doors marked janitorial and electrical access. Lenny felt he had seen too many hallways since starting this job. He imagined this one, like all the others, hid more than it seemed. They were probably walking straight toward another trap.

And why not? It was much easier to have him walk than to be dragged somewhere.

Lenny wished Terrifitemps had taught him some basic martial arts moves, or given him a lighter that doubled as a blowtorch. Maybe those would come later in his orientation. The crisis had come on his first day of work, and he had been thrown out into the field and, ultimately, into the hands of the enemy.

Foo stopped abruptly. "Turn here." A portion of the wall shifted silently aside, revealing a large, mostly empty room. As far as Lenny could tell, the only object in the room was Sheila, still tied to a chair. Lenny ran across the worn carpet, straight to her side.

"Sheila?" he called as he looked down at the complicated knots wound around the back of the chair.

She spat out her gag. "You're alone?"

Lenny waved at the hooded figure who marched toward them. "Foo brought me here."

Sheila nodded, apparently satisfied. "Good. I don't need any of this anymore." She stood, the ropes falling away around her.

"I hope you weren't too uncomfortable." Foo stepped to Lenny's side. "My little princess."

Sheila kissed Foo's cheek. "Could you give us some time alone, Daddy?"

Lenny stared.

Daddy?

Eleven

Foo did not look at all pleased.
"Time is of the essence!" he insisted. "We need to talk logistics!"
Sheila looked at Foo. Lenny knew that look. Foo stood his ground.
"Daddy?" she said. Lenny also knew that tone of voice.
Foo took a step back. He knew that voice, too. He held up his hands in surrender.
"All right, dear. We'll give you a minute."
Sheila continued to stare at her father.
"I divine," Swami Phil announced, "that these two would prefer to be left alone."
Foo looked the slightest bit cross. Bruno continued to glower. The swami shooed both of them from the room.
Lenny took a good look at Sheila. And she did look good. Her blonde hair was cut in an attractive bob that framed her face, and all those ropes and gags had not smudged her impeccable makeup or creased her low-cut evening gown. Lenny had never seen Sheila dressed so formally.
The door slid shut behind the others. The two of them stood there in silence. Lenny didn't know what to say. Sheila smiled as though she might be the slightest bit embarrassed.
She took a deep breath before she began. "I suppose there are a few teensy things I never told you about me."
"Few?" Lenny asked. "Teensy?"
He studied the woman who stood before him. What did he really know about Sheila? She had worked in advertising back when they were dating. He had even been to a Christmas party at her office. He wondered now if the ad agency had just been another front for Foo.
"This is somewhat bigger than teensy." Lenny waved at the very large room, and all the rooms beyond. "Why didn't you tell me about any of this?"

"Would you have understood?" Sheila asked with a scowl. "How does someone describe a father like Foo? Let me tell you, it's not easy being the daughter of an international criminal mastermind!"

Lenny guessed she had a point. But what else did he know about her past—or what did he think he knew? Back when they were together, Sheila had told him about a childhood spent in boarding school, followed by four years at a small college in Ohio. She hadn't dated since her college boyfriend had met with a tragic accident. It was only now Lenny thought to question the details of her boyfriend's death.

On their first few dates, Sheila had spent a lot of time asking about him. And he was happy to talk. He had dated girls on and off from late in high school, but Sheila was the first one who would really listen. He had felt an instant connection. They seemed to enjoy a lot of the same things—movies, games, nights out with friends—at least at first. Lenny had had other relationships before, but this was the first one where everything felt right. They just fit together—Sheila pushed Lenny forward when he dug in his heels, while he held Sheila back when she got a bit too impulsive. And it had worked, until it didn't.

Thinking about it now, maybe he had opened up a bit more than he should have. And why hadn't he asked more questions about Sheila?

Lenny felt a cool pressure against his fingers. Sheila had taken his hand. In her fashionable heels, she was almost as tall as he was. She looked him in the eyes.

"I know we ended badly. I know the things I said. Like we weren't meant for each other. Like you had no ambition. Like you would never do anything with your life. Like I couldn't be seen going out with a man whose life was becoming a joke. Like I couldn't let on that people were laughing at you behind your back!" She looked up to the ceiling, as though she could barely contain the emotions welling up inside her. "And like you always let the dishes pile up in the sink."

She squeezed his hand with a sigh, and looked Lenny straight in the eye. Lenny had always thought her eyes were a very nice shade of blue. "But I was wrong."

Lenny and Sheila just stood there for a long moment. She had told him people were laughing at him? He had forgotten that part.

Sheila spoke first. "Well, maybe I wasn't wrong about the dishes, but still, look at you now."

Sheila was an attractive woman, especially when she was smiling. And yet, looking at her, Lenny remembered all the fights they'd had at the end of the relationship. After a while, no matter what he said, it was wrong, wrong, wrong. Seeing Sheila smile, a part of Lenny wanted to forget all about the past. But how long would that smile last?

"You have finally found a job perfectly suited to your skills," Sheila said. "For the first time, you have a real chance of success." She increased the pressure on his hand. "It should be obvious that I find this very attractive."

Lenny took a deep breath. "I'm flattered. But there were a lot of reasons that we broke up."

Sheila's smile faltered ever so slightly. "You never did listen. I'm on your side. I've always been on your side. Why else would I want to get to know you so well?"

Lenny realized a bit of his old anger was coming back. "It was different when we were first getting to know each other. But then you stopped asking how I felt about things and just started telling me what to do. My job wasn't good enough. We needed a better place to live. Why didn't we get away more on weekends?"

Sheila's smile faltered. "Are you saying I ordered you around?"

"Well, yes."

"I was only looking out for your best interests!"

"Sure, as you saw them."

"And that's why you got so angry? It would have been nice if you had explained that to me—back when it happened." Her voice got louder with every word. "A relationship is a two-way street. If you're still not bright enough to know that, maybe we don't get back together after all!"

"Fine with me! Until you showed up, I hadn't thought about you in months!" As soon as Lenny had said that, he realized his words weren't totally true. But they sure sounded good and angry.

"Even better for me!" she snapped. This was the Sheila he remembered well. "When I think of all the time I've wasted thinking about you, dreaming about the two of us together." She wiped away a single tear. "With you, I thought world domination could be something really special! But it's the same old problem. I would have had to explain my father."

Sheila sighed. "There are no winners here. You're still impossible! How could I ever think I could change you?"

Before Lenny could come up with a suitably angry reply, he heard a soft knock on the door. Foo and his two cohorts reentered the room.

"Have you come to your decision?" Sheila's father asked as they approached.

Sheila gave Lenny a single glance before she replied. "I'm sorry, Daddy. I think we're going to have to kill him after all."

"Wait a minute!" Lenny shouted. When did a lover's squabble end in death? "Just because we don't agree on some things is no reason—"

Sheila gave him one of those looks that cut him off midsentence. "It is a bit abrupt, I'll admit. But what else can I do?" She brightened, ever so slightly. "I know! Lenny, would you like to choose how you'll die? For all you've been through, it's the least I can do."

"So he gets to choose his destruction?" Foo asked. "Most generous!" He turned to regard Lenny. "Very well, young Mr. Hodge. What's your poison? The room of a thousand knives? The mind-alteration lab? Torture Suite B?" When Lenny didn't reply, Foo turned back to his daughter. "Sheila? Any suggestions?"

She hesitated a moment before she answered. "I was leaning toward the shark tank. He needs to suffer."

"Now, Sheila?" Lenny had to take control. "Maybe I was too hasty. We've always fought. But remember what came after that? It was always better when we made up again."

Her face showed the hint of a smile. "You're right. Sometimes I can be a little impatient."

Sometimes? Sort of like Niagara Falls sometimes has running water. Lenny did his best to keep on smiling.

Sheila nodded. "Okay, he doesn't have to suffer that much. I think it's the reptile den, Daddy." Her smile grew as she thought of her decision. "It will be quick—well, quicker."

"Very well." Foo grinned at Lenny. "Don't be so worried, Mr. Hodge. With the reptiles, you have a choice. Will the Komodo dragon get you first, or it could be the giant crocodile, or even the poisonous black mamba snake? Think of it as an adventure."

"Bruno?" Foo nodded to the large man at his side. "If you would accompany Mr. Hodge? Now that Sheila has made her decision, we don't want to tarry."

Lenny looked at the man lumbering toward him. How could he fight against that? Maybe he could move faster than Bruno, dodge his grasp, and make a run for it.

Lenny ducked, and found his head firmly held by a very large hand. Another hand grabbed his belt.

"But—" Lenny began as the large man simply picked him up and carried him.

"We'll be coming along," Foo said by Bruno's side. "We may be taking you to your death, but at least you'll have an appreciative audience."

How could this be happening? Lenny had to do something. But what?

Lenny heard a burst of Wagner's "Der Ring des Nibelungen." Foo pulled out his cell phone.

"What?" Foo barked. "How is that possible?"

He looked at the others. "Apparently our direct route to the reptile pit is blocked. What is it?" He said to the phone.

He looked back to the others with a frown. "Apparently the hall outside is jammed with a herd of buffalo."

He turned back to the phone. "What? Not just a herd of buffalo? Oh. I see." He looked at the others. "This is no ordinary herd. The bison are all wearing uniforms. Red jackets with brass buttons. And they're singing."

"Singing?" Sheila stepped in front of Lenny. "This is your fault!"

Lenny blinked. Apparently, it was.

Twelve

Foo's mouth actually fell open as he stared down the hallway. "This is totally preposterous!

Sheila nodded. "Welcome to my world. Well, Lenny's world, actually. I was only visiting. But, this is not much stranger than—well, a lot of things."

Actually, Lenny thought, this one is up there with the tap-dancing toads. He was oddly calm in the face of this. Despite the fact that he had tried not to think too much about these surprises in his life, he had more or less come to accept them. Compared to whatever waited for him in the reptile room, those singing buffalo seemed positively comforting.

The wide corridor before them was packed with a large number of buffalo. Just your ordinary very large, very hairy mammals—Lenny had seen some of them at a Western theme park when he was a kid—except that each of these large animals was wearing what? A team jacket? The clothes were draped over the animals something like a horse blanket, if that blanket were to have short sleeves to cover the top of the bison's forelegs, and if that blanket was made out of some shiny, dark-red material. A large yellow "B" was emblazoned on every one. And there were, indeed, brass buttons on the corners.

The bison snorted and grunted and made low rumbling noises as Lenny and the others approached.

"What should we do?" Foo murmured. "I was so looking forward to the reptile room."

"There's only one way to approach this," Sheila replied. "We have to give them Lenny."

"No reptiles?" Her father sighed. "Very well. I suppose death by buffalo stampede will have to do."

Foo stepped aside. Bruno pushed Lenny to the front of the group.

The satin-jacketed buffalo noticed immediately. Their snorting and shuffling increased in intensity. Lenny wondered if Foo's secret headquarters could withstand the onrushing herd.

"Whatever is going to happen," Sheila said, "it will happen now."

Lenny stared at the mass of animals crammed in the corridor before him.

And something changed.

It began with a sort of a moooo mumble sound, as a low rumble spread across through herd. A louder voice came from somewhere at the center of the crowd. "One, two, three!"

With that, the bison began to sing.

Pack up your troubles in your old kit-bag,
And smile, smile, smile!

"They're singing!" Swami Phil cried with delight. "And in harmony!"

"They're not only singing, they're also not moving!" Foo was not so pleased.

The bison continued with growing enthusiasm:

What's the use of worrying?
It never was worthwhile, so
Pack up your—

Swami Phil regarded the buffalo a bit more skeptically than before. "We have ways of getting around this."

The words snapped Foo back to attention. "The swami is correct. This place was built to my specifications. I planned for everything." He studied a wall panel filled with random decorative tiles. "Even the secret passages have secret passages—"

His voice faded as *"And smile, smile, smile!"* thundered down the hall.

The bison paused. Foo looked sharply at Lenny, as though he were the cause of all this. Well, actually, Lenny supposed he might be, if he could ever figure out how these strange events happened. The silence stretched on. Lenny waited, almost afraid to breathe.

The herd stirred. Quiet moos turned to murmurs. And then a voice from the center shouted:

"A-one and a-two!"

The furry chorus responded in unison.

It's a long way to Tipperary,
It's a long way to go.

"It will never end, will it?" Foo asked. "This corridor will always be filled with singing buffalo." He took a deep breath. "But I have other corridors! Let these buffalo sing forever!" He felt along the wall. "It should be just about here."

The criminal mastermind pressed a yellow tile with an embossed yet abstract squiggle. Maybe it was meant to be a butterfly. Or a flower. Or just a squiggle. It was hard to tell.

A door slid open as the bison's song rose in intensity.

To the sweetest girl I know.
Good-bye, Piccadilly!
Farewell, Leicester Square!
It's a long, long way to Tipperary—

Foo rushed through the door, waving the others to follow. Lenny found himself carried out of the hall as the door shut soundly behind them.

"The sooner we're away from here . . ." Foo took a deep breath. The bison's song carried faintly through the wall. "Well, it's all right now. With all that noise I couldn't think."

But the bison had made Lenny thoughtful in a completely different way. This chaos was helping him. Maybe Ms. Siggenbottom really was right, and these events would lead not to Lenny's death, but his freedom.

Foo led the rest of the party down a wide staircase carpeted in royal blue. At the foot of the stairs were row on row of machines of a sort even Lenny recognized. Most of them were game consoles—the kind found in arcades, with the occasional pinball and Whack-A-Gator machine to break up the lineup of Space Invaders, Tetris and race-car games. Above the dozens of consoles, two of the three large flat-screen TVs showed the Super Mario Bros. and Ms. Pac-Man leaping around in incredible high definition, while a soldier tediously mowed down zombies on the third.

"One of our secret recreation areas," Foo explained as they descended the stairs.

"Wow." Lenny was impressed, despite himself. There must be hundreds of arcade games down here, many dating back to his childhood.

"This is what impresses you?" Only Sheila could put that much disdain in her voice. "Typical."

"We have everything," Foo continued as if his daughter hadn't spoken. "Not that we have much time to use them. World conquest is a full-time business." Besides the many games, the room was empty.

They reached the bottom of the stairs, but Lenny kept walking. He found himself attracted to one machine in particular.

"And where do you think you're—" Sheila began.

"No—" Swami Phil interrupted. "Let him go. This is part of his gift."

Lenny walked up to a fortune-telling machine, a box shaped like a booth, with brightly painted words on the front: what is your future? secrets revealed!

Above the bright letters was a glassed-in square, showing a plaster head and shoulders of a bearded man in a turban. He looked a bit like Swami Phil.

"I come from a long line of swamis," Phil said before anyone could ask.

Before Lenny touched the machine, it made a soft whirring sound and discharged a small square of paper. Phil grabbed the scrap before it could fall to the floor.

He read it aloud.

"Pong holds your future."

"Pong?" Sheila asked. "What is pong?"

"Pong!" a deep voice called from the far corner of the room.

"We have to investigate," Phil said.

Sheila rolled her eyes. "Why not? It's not as if we were in a rush to dispose of this man! While we're at it, why don't we give him a retirement plan and a 401(k)?"

"Now dear," Foo replied. "This may be part of something bigger."

"You're so self-centered!" Sheila glanced petulantly at Lenny. "You won't let me have the slightest little revenge!"

Lenny resisted the urge to shrug and grin. It wasn't as if he were planning any of this.

"Pong!" came once again from the corner. Lenny walked toward the sound. The others followed.

Lenny recognized the squat, gray machine from three rows away. The green screen showed the action of a simulated game, a bright light sent back and forth, propelled by other lights intercepting it on either side of the screen. Pong was the first and simplest of the video games, basically ping-pong played in two dimensions. Still, Lenny had loved it, way back when.

"It doesn't look like much," Sheila sniffed.

"Pong!" the machine replied defiantly.

"The fortune-teller said it held the future," the swami said. Lenny walked over to the game.

HELLO LENNY! appeared on the screen.

"Hello," Lenny replied. It was the polite response, after all.

"What good is an ancient game machine?" Foo demanded.

I CAN TELL YOUR FUTURE scrolled across the screen. OR MAYBE I CAN PREVENT IT.

"This is nonsense!" Foo fumed.

"There is no nonsense," Swami Phil replied calmly. "Only fate."

"Only fate?" Sheila asked. "And what does that mean?"

The swami shrugged. "Sounds good, doesn't it?"

"Pong!" the game interrupted.

LOOK AT THE LARGE SCREEN ABOVE THE GAME'S SCREEN scrolled across its monitor.

Lenny and the others looked up to the large video displays. They were filled with what looked like an architectural schematic shown in green lines on a black background.

The criminal mastermind gasped. "It's a map of my secret headquarters!"

INDEED Pong agreed. IN PRESENT TIME. OBSERVE. HALL TO YOUR LEFT, FLOODED. Two lines to the left of the screen became one solid green block. FILLED WITH MAN-EATING FISH.

"There must have been a breach in the Aquarium of Death!" Phil exclaimed.

Pong continued. HALL TO YOUR RIGHT BLOCKED BY MUTANT POISON IVY. LOTS OF POISON IVY. IMPASSABLE POISON IVY. The corridor to the right of the screen became a solid green block, as well.

"It must have spread from our Greenhouse Weapons Center!" Phil conjectured.

YOU HAVE NOWHERE TO GO.

"Nonsense!" Foo replied. "We have not even begun to exploit my secret secret passages!" He punched a red button above the Pong machine. A door slid aside.

". . . pass the ammunition, and we'll allll stayyy freeee!" came the chorus from the other side. The door slid shut.

"How can the buffalo be in my secret corridors?" Foo whispered. "It's Lenny, isn't it?"

"Pong!" the game agreed.

Lenny took a deep breath. He was feeling the usual lack of control—panic, really—that overtook him whenever these events began. Facing death by reptile was one thing, at least you knew what you were getting into. This, on the other hand—

"Isn't there somewhere we can go?" he asked.

ALL SITES THAT LEAD TO LENNY'S DEATH HAVE BEEN NULLIFIED. THERE IS STILL ONE WAY OUT.

The three giant video monitors displayed arrows pointing down and to the left. Lenny turned and saw a large red exit sign about fifty feet away.

"Thank you," Lenny said.

THANK YOU, LENNY, the screen scrolled. THE OTHER GAMES MADE FUN OF ME, BUT I KNEW MY TIME WOULD COME AGAIN. PONG NEVER GIVES UP HO–

Bruno lifted Lenny from the ground and carried him toward the exit sign.

Swami Phil shouted in surprise.

"Look! The floor in front of the exit! The carpet's covered by rats!"

Lenny blinked in surprise, a newfound hopefulness rising inside him. The rodents stopped scampering around in front of him, and lined up in three neat rows facing Lenny. A hundred high, squeaky voices spoke as one:

There was a young man who was stuck,
And thought he was plumb out of luck!
But he knew a crew
Who were honest and true
Who said "Lenny, you'd better duck!"

"What does that mean?" Foo demanded.

"Never mind," Sheila called from up ahead. "The rats are scattering. We have a clear path to the door."

Once again, Lenny felt himself lifted and carried forward. But Bruno stopped his headlong rush mere feet from the exit.

Someone was knocking on the door from the other side.

Thirteen

The door was flung open with such force that even Bruno was thrown to the ground. Lenny fell on top of the large man as two shadowy men in raincoats stepped into the game room. The Dimm had returned.

Lenny took a deep breath. He was shaken but not hurt. Bruno groaned beneath him, where he had cushioned Lenny's fall.

What were the Dimm doing here? After the rhyming rats, Lenny was sure he'd see his Terrifitemps team on the other side of that door. But he saw only the Dimm, clad in raincoats and shadows.

"How dare you interfere!" Foo shouted as the two moved silently into the room.

One of them strode up to Foo. The shadows followed, obscuring the game consoles to either side. "We do apologize. This would have been over long ago, if not for the nature of our subject's power."

"There is no doubt now this Lenny Hodge is the one," the other added from his position by the door. As if to prove the Dimm's point, Lenny heard the distant sounds of the buffalo chorus singing "The Yellow Rose of Texas."

"No more World War One fighting songs?" Swami Phil smiled beatifically as he tapped his foot to the buffalo chorus. "They've started singing Americana!"

"We need the man who brought them here." The Dimm who had confronted Foo turned to regard Lenny and Bruno, both just pushing themselves off the floor. "Lenny Hodge, you cannot escape your destiny."

The swami stepped forward to block the Dimm's path.

"Pardon me, but what exactly is Lenny's destiny?"

"And who might you be?" asked the Dimm by the door.

"I am Swami Phil," he said with a slight bow. "I know the secrets of the East. Also the secrets of the West and South, although there's not as much call for those. I'm still working on the secrets of the North. A fellow has to have a hobby, after all."

The Dimm's shadow crept across the swami. Phil's smile faltered ever so slightly. "The short answer," he added quickly, "is I am the greatest seer I know, and whatever is going on with this fellow"—he waved both hands at Lenny—"is completely beyond me."

"We have no need of swamis. If you would step aside?" Both Dimm grunted as one, as if dismissing the swami from further consideration. Then the shadow men turned toward Lenny. "You have no means of escape."

The Dimm glided in Lenny's direction. No one moved to stop them. The Dimm towered over everyone. They grew more direct, more powerful. Even their shadows were longer than before. They paused, side by side, half a dozen paces from Lenny.

"You have eluded us before. We can take no more chances." The two spoke as one. "We were forced to call in our supervisor."

Lenny looked up to see—something else—walk through the door.

If the Dimm were difficult to see, their superior was entirely beyond comprehension—a rolling mass of darkness that Lenny found impossible to focus on. His gaze kept shifting elsewhere, to Sheila and the swami, quaking with apprehension, as if they saw death; to Foo, red in the face, as if he might explode with anger; and finally to Bruno, who reached inside his vest to pull out a gun.

"Please," a voice boomed from within the darkness. "No more interference."

Bruno wasn't listening. He aimed his snub-nosed revolver and fired three quick shots. All three bullets disappeared in the darkness that might be the supervisor of the Dimm.

The voice once again came from within the total lack of light. "We are sorry it has come to this."

Bruno gasped, a sudden look of panic in his eye. He turned his head to Foo. "Master," he began, "I—" But his voice was choked off as he was lifted from the floor. He thrashed in midair, his face turning blue as he gasped for air. His eyes closed, and he was tossed to the floor.

"He will recover," the voice boomed from the darkness. "This time!"

Lenny glanced down at the large man. Bruno had passed out, but he was still breathing.

"We do not kill people," the unseen supervisor continued. "Unless, of course, it is necessary."

The darkness swirled about the entry to the room. "Now, Lenny Hodge, you must accept your fate. My operatives, P79K43 and 8Y87G4, have brought me here, because they are incapable of securing you for our purposes. Therefore, I will finish the job." The darkness rolled in Lenny's direction. "Prepare to be enveloped."

Foo studied the empty blackness before him. "You are displeased with your subordinates?"

The darkness hesitated a moment before answering. "No matter how much you train them—"

"Say no more." Foo nodded in agreement. "Your underlings will always disappoint you."

"Dad!" Sheila called. "How can you say that? Bruno almost died for you!"

Foo only sighed. "It's always almost, isn't it?"

"And you two!" the darkness rumbled. "I do not pay you to stand around. Do not forget, we have a second task."

One of the underlings turned and glided toward Sheila. The young woman glared at his approach.

The thing in the raincoat stopped a foot before her face. "You cannot hide from the Dimm. Where have you hidden the first day cover?"

For the first time since Lenny had found her in Foo's lair, Sheila looked truly alarmed. "What are you talking about?"

"We were there, at Lenny Hodge's living area, only a minute too late. The Dimm know all."

Sheila seemed stunned into silence.

Really? Lenny thought. He remembered looking at his stamp collection and realizing the most valuable stamp of all was missing. Sheila was the thief? That surprised him as much as anything that had happened since he'd started this job. Sure, Sheila said she wanted to kill him. But he never thought she'd mess with his stamp collection.

Foo responded for his daughter. "Ah, so there is something you want as well? Perhaps we can make some compromise."

"The Dimm let nothing deter them from their goals." The darkness boomed dismissively.

"As you should! But you haven't really taken a look at my organization. It's one lean, mean fighting machine! Both of us want to rule the world. Perhaps we could even talk—merger?" He sidled over to the darkness, talking in a subdued voice.

Lenny backed slowly away from the discussion. So now they both planned to capture and kill him. And that was pretty much all that was happening. Shouldn't his gift be kicking in just about now? He thought again about what the mysterious S had told him. He had to be proactive about these things, and help his gift along. Maybe he could find a secret passageway of his own.

Bruno groaned and shook his head, blinking at the ever-changing lights on the games nearby. Everybody else in the room was watching Foo and the black void. They had forgotten about Lenny.

Maybe this was his gift after all.

The darkness raised its voice loud enough for all to hear. "We have no need of your death traps and doomsday devices!"

Foo took a step away from the void. It continued, "We will find out where this Lenny gets his strange abilities. But be assured. We are under strict orders. We only dissect him as a last resort."

"Dissection?" Foo raised a single eyebrow.

"We only want to learn his secrets," the chief Dimm explained. You can have him back when we're done. Or, at least, whatever pieces remain."

Foo nodded, resigned to Lenny's fate. "Then I suppose Sheila will have her revenge, if only from a distance." He glanced at his daughter. "Although I think we all would have preferred the reptile room."

Enough of this! Just because this void with a booming voice wanted to take Lenny didn't mean he had to give himself up. Lenny dodged around the nearest game console, which sported a steering wheel and made revving engine and squealing brake noises. He headed for the opposite corner of the room.

"And where do you think you're going?" the rolling darkness asked. "There is no escape. My reach is everywhere."

Lenny backed away through the maze of gaming machines. The darkness pursued him.

Something fell with a resounding crash.

"Ow," the darkness remarked. "You're only delaying the inevitable. Surely, my cloak of darkness can obscure my surroundings a bit, but your strange power shines through it like a beacon. "It will only take a moment to be enveloped." The void rolled forward. "Once you're absorbed, you won't feel a thing. Well, unless we have to do that dissection. But rest assured, we start out by cutting off the smallest little bits. You'll barely notice some of them are gone." Something else crashed to the floor. "Ow! Of course, if you are stubborn about your secret we will need to dig deeper—"

The void was interrupted by yet another crash. "Who put these machines so close together? Please remain still, Mr. Hodge. Moving will only prolong the agony. The supervisor of the Dimm is above such petty physical concerns."

Lenny slowly continued to back away, past a mechanical horse and a pinball machine playing some jaunty TV theme. He was careful not to trip on any of the mechanisms himself, then half hid behind a sign reading EVERYONE WINS AT SKEE BALL!

Two more crashes in quick succession. "Ow. Ow. Ow. Shouldn't there be a pathway? Are these machines on wheels? What sort of sadist set up this room in the first place?"

As if to answer the Dimm's question, a single machine voice rang out from amid the games.

"Pong!"

Fourteen

"Ow!" the darkness cried again.
The answering word rose from the forest of consoles.
"Pong!"
Then, from another corner of the room.
"Pong!"
All the machines began to beep and chatter, as if urging the Pong machine onward.
"Beep click click beep," a console to his left announced.
"Korgar," a pinball machine to his right replied.
The sound bounced on from game to game.
"Beep beep honk beep."
"Kung Fu Fighter!"
"Beep de beep de beep beep beep!"
"Pong!"
Lenny's gift had been working all the time. The games would give him a chance to escape. He slid between a Whack-A-Gator and a Ms. Pac-Man.
"Help me, Dimm!" the dark supervisor cried. "We cannot allow our prey to escape!"
"Certainly sir." One of the two raincoated Dimm approached on Lenny's right.
"Our pleasure!" The other swung through the game consoles to Lenny's left.
The beeping noises grew ever louder. Beep honk bleep jingle. A male voice shouting, "Play Blackjack!" Beep ayooga beep beep crash. It was the sound of triumph, a battle cry for gaming consoles everywhere. And, above it all, that one repeated word:
"Pong! Pong! Pon . . ." The cry faded as quickly as it had come.
"I just had to find the plug," the void said. "Now if Mr. Hodge would kindly remain still? It is time for me to envelop and be gone." A great

darkness reared up before Lenny.

With another great boom of wood hitting wall, the door to the game room flew open one more time.

Lenny hadn't realized somebody had closed the door in the first place. He was still very happy to see who stood on the other side.

"You go no farther!" Karnowski the Ghost Finder declared. "Terrifitemps is here!"

"See?" someone insubstantial added. Lenny squinted and made out the nameless ghost from the pit.

"I told you I could find this place again!" the ghost continued. "They don't call me—well, actually, they don't call me anything."

Foo stared at the newcomers with an angry frown. "Is my secret lair a secret to anybody?"

"You will give us Lenny now," the Baron added, "or I will release the rats."

"And I will befuddle you with my legions of spirits," Karnowski said.

"I will use my mental powers to discern and foil all of your plans," Lenore added.

"Ignore them!" the dark void commanded from the other side of the room. "Our only priority is the capture of Mr. Hodge!"

"Yes sir!" one of his underlings barked.

"We live to obey," the other remarked. The two Dimm pushed forward to either side of their leader. Lenny found himself pinned in the corner, with only half a dozen game consoles between him and the encroaching darkness.

The Baron howled and waved his cape. "Come, my brethren!"

Lenny recognized the gray carpet sweeping across the floor.

"Watch out!" Swami Phil called.

"Ewww!" Sheila remarked with disdain. "Rats? I won't put up with rats. Here! I'll kick them away with my pointy toes." The rodents squealed as she did just that. "I knew these fashion heels would serve a purpose!"

Karnowski raised his closed fist high in the air. "Attack, O spirits!"

"Oooooooh!" the nameless ghost moaned. Other, fainter groans and shrieks gathered around him.

Bruno waved his gun around. "Boss! Who do you want me to shoot next?"

Foo pointed past the Dimm. "Plug anybody who tries to take Hodge from the room."

"Ooooooooooh?" the ghost tried again. More shrieks, more groans, but, even without the Pong machine, they had trouble being heard over the incessant game console chatter.

"Lenny!" Lenore shouted. "Don't lose hope. We'll get to you somehow!"

"You do not steal my victim from my lair!" Foo was so angry he didn't notice the rodents scurrying inside his robes.

"I have had enough of outside interference. Lenny Hodge is going to die when and where we decide!"

"Now that's the Daddy Foo I remember!" Sheila cried out as she kicked a rat across the room.

"Ignore these people!" the booming void demanded. "Ignore these games, and ghosts, and rodents, and anything else they throw at us. The Dimm will not be defeated!"

"As you say, Wise One," the Dimm on the void's left answered.

"Right on the money with that one, Chief," the other Dimm echoed.

"Would you mind," asked Bruno, a pleading tone in his voice, "if I shot a few vermin?"

"Ooooh? Ooh ooh ooh? Anybody?" The ghost paused to wipe nonexistent sweat from his nonexistent brow. "Boy, this is a tough room. I knew I should have brought my chains!"

"Come, my rats!" the Baron cried from where he stood just inside the door. "Scamper as though your very lives depend upon it!"

"Come, my spirits!" Karnowski added with verve. "Chill these souls. Show them what it means to be truly dead!"

"This isn't working as well as I had hoped," Lenore admitted. "We have to find a distraction. Where's a werevole when you need one?"

"Listen!" Swami Phil called above the constant din. "Aren't the buffalo getting closer?"

Lenny listened. Yes! He could hear it, too. There, just beyond the gaming beeps and ghostly moans, a great chorus admired the Yellow Rose of Texas.

"We must take him now!" Even the void was beginning to sound desperate. "Hold Mr. Hodge firmly. He must be enveloped for the good of the Dimm!"

The two Dimm in raincoats lunged forward to grab Lenny as an even louder crash than any he had heard before came from directly behind him.

Everyone froze.

Lenny coughed as he turned around and got a face full of dust.

"Be careful, my minions!" Foo called from the middle of the room. "My advanced air-filtration system will soon show us just what has happened."

Lenny heard the whoosh of giant fans as the view went from impenetrable to slightly hazy in a matter of seconds. The wall behind him was gone. In its place stood another wall, a tall, furry wall composed of over two dozen buffalo, crammed side by side along the entire length of the new opening.

And the buffalo sang:

Swanee, how I love you, how I love you
My dear old Swanee,
I'd pay the world to see . . .

"Singing buffalo?" Lenore asked. "Now, there's a distraction!"

"It is impressive," the swami agreed. "And I don't think we've heard their full repertoire."

"It will do you no good, Mr. Hodge." Irritation crept into the void's voice. "Envelopment, dissection, it will all still go according to schedule. But now we'll have musical accompaniment."

"Oh yeah?" Lenny started, but could think of nothing else to add. Like many of the things that happened around him, the bison chorus was strange and spectacular and pretty much totally passive. Stampeding buffalo he might be able to use; singing buffalo, not so much. The jaunty chorus did make Foo's secret lair a bit more cheerful, though.

"Lenny?" Sheila asked. "So you brought the buffalo?"

He was startled by her question. How could he explain a power he didn't really understand?

"Kind of—I suppose so—yeah," he finally admitted.

Sheila sighed and shook her head. "You know, until this minute, I could never admit to myself how strange you really were."

"Lenny?" Lenore stared hard at Sheila. "This is your old girlfriend."

He found himself genuinely surprised. "Huh? How could you know that?"

"Our files on you are very extensive," Karnowski explained.

"They did not mention that she was in league with Foo," Lenore said.

"His daughter, actually," Lenny added.

Karnowski grunted. "Our files are not extensive enough."

"Did the files tell you why we broke up?" Sheila demanded. "Did the files tell you that Lenny loved his stamp collection more than me?"

That wasn't true at all, Lenny thought. How could Sheila ever make that comparison? Then again, he could remember very few screaming arguments with his first day covers.

"No," Lenore replied, "our files tell us about the real Lenny Hodge." Her stare became even harder than before. "Sheila? That is your name, right? You'll never know what you lost when you left Lenny. You'll never know what you had. Lenny's in a safer place now. With Terrifitemps, we'll see to his happiness in ways you could never imagine."

Lenny realized he was smiling. He really liked when Lenore said something supportive like that. He hadn't had that many people really try to understand him. He wondered—with that mention of happiness—if she was speaking for herself, or for Terrifitemps?

He glanced to his right and saw the void rearing up before him. Why was he thinking about Lenore when he was about to be cut into little pieces?

But, rather than enveloping him, the Dimm supervisor spoke. "We have already spent far too long in the pursuit of Lenny Hodge." The darkness twisted about. "Foo. Perhaps we can come to an agreement. What do you want from this individual?"

The criminal mastermind smiled with great satisfaction, as if he had been waiting for someone to ask this very question. "We simply wanted to destroy all of Terrifitemps to clear the way for our total global synergy. Lenny just seemed like a particularly strong piece of the puzzle."

"Such a pitiful goal," the void rumbled in response, "when the Dimm could offer you so much more."

Foo paused to stare at the floor for a moment. He sighed and looked up at his daughter.

"I'm sorry, Sheila, but a quick death, or at least a quickish death for Lenny, seems terribly shortsighted. Rather than continue this discord, I believe we should not further hinder in the Dimm's examination—and dissection." He waved vaguely at the void. "You may take him. We will not stop you."

"Finally!" the swirling darkness cried in triumph. "If you two would hold him?"

But the void's subordinates hesitated. The room was suddenly very quiet. The bison had finished their song.

And then, from the middle of the herd: "Uno, dos!"

And the buffalo began again. *"La-la-la-la-la la bamba!"*

The room shook as the bison tapped their right forehooves in time. The menacing void stumbled backward.

"*Y arriba arriba!*" the bison continued.

"Do I hear music?" a cheerful voice cried out.

Something large and blue materialized in their midst.

"Bob?" Lenny asked.

"Bob the horse!" another dozen voices called as one. It seemed that just about everyone knew the pooka. Lenny could swear he'd even heard Bob's name uttered by a couple of the game consoles.

Bob grinned at everyone in the room. "Boy, am I glad to see you guys! I haven't had anybody to talk to in, like, forever!"

"What is this final annoyance?" the void demanded.

The two Dimm exchanged shadowed glances.

"You don't know Bob?" both asked as one.

"And I don't want to know him, either." The void was growing irritable. "Will these distractions never end? Stop him from getting any closer!"

Bob cantered about, midair. "Here I was, dancing to a cha-cha beat. Those Latin rhythms are the best! One, two, one-two-three. And then where do I end up? Nowhere! I was in the middle of the Big Empty!"

"I can't concentrate!" the void rumbled. "Get him away from me!"

"What was that you said, Boss?" one of the Dimm replied.

"It's getting awfully difficult to hear with all this noise, Your Honor," the other one added.

"*La-la-la-la-la la bamba,*" the buffalo chorus added.

"I wonder who got me into this in the first place?" Bob continued cheerfully. "He could use a good talking to! And I'm just the pooka to do it!"

Lenny saw Swami Phil quietly back out of the room.

"Enough!" the void insisted. "I need you to deal with that blue thing so I can get back to enveloping."

One of his subordinates shook his shadowy head. "I'm sorry sir. I can't hear you over all that singing. What thing that blew in here are you talking about?"

"Nothing that blew in!" the void insisted. "I'm talking about that blue horse!"

"You will get hoarse if you keep shouting like that," the other Dimm agreed. "I don't think we can talk in here at all, Boss. Maybe we can have this conversation out in the hall."

"The hall it is," the first junior Dimm agreed all too readily. He called out to the void: "We'll meet you whenever you're done doing whatever you need to do in here."

The two Dimm nodded cheerfully and made a pronounced detour around Bob as they ran for the door.

Bob barely seemed to notice. "I don't know where I'd be without your buffalo singers. The minute I heard 'La Bamba,' I knew I was going home!"

The void thrashed about in midair. "Where did they go? No matter. I don't need any help from my underlings!"

Bob whinnied cheerfully. "I really owe you one. Lenny, we're going to be best friends forever!"

"La-la bamba, la-la bamba!"

"I was enveloping victims before they were born!" the void shouted at no one in particular. "I can take a little pressure. I'll show them what a supervisor can do!"

Bob the horse cocked his head to one side, as if only now noticing the void. "What's up with this guy?"

Lenny shouted a brief description of the whole enveloping/dismemberment scenario as best he could over the singing buffalo, who were now keeping time with both forelegs.

Bob nodded as if he understood perfectly. "See? I told you things were going to get worse. Always trust a pooka!" He turned to the rolling blackness. "Maybe this cloud guy and I need to have a little talk."

"Envelop! Absorb!" the void screamed. "Smash! Kill!"

Lenny wasn't so sure that was a good idea. "But what if—"

"Nonsense. Pookas are welcome everywhere! Maybe I can teach him a few dance moves."

Bob reared onto his hind legs. With a shout of "Hola!" he galloped headfirst into the void.

Fifteen

The buffalo were silent at last. The noise from the games seemed to have diminished, as if Bob's departure had sucked the energy from the room. Even the void was nearly silent, emitting a muffled sigh or groan now and then, as though having a particularly bad dream or a bit of indigestion.

Lenny saw no sign of Bob the horse. Apparently the pooka had been enveloped, at least for now. Lenny was sure Bob would fare far better than he would have. How the heck could even the Dimm dissect a pooka?

"Now should I shoot somebody?" Bruno asked, shattering the stillness.

Foo surveyed the game room for an instant before he shook his head. "The situation has changed. It is not the time to confront our enemies directly." He clapped his hands sharply.

"A good leader knows when to cut and run. Minions! Into the photo booth!"

Sheila, Bruno, and Foo were joined by a pair in red robes who must have been skulking behind the game consoles. They passed one by one through a curtain under a sign that read: 4 photos for $10.

Lenny heard a loud grinding noise overhead the instant the last of Foo's group disappeared through the curtain. A hatchway opened in the ceiling directly over the photo booth, and the booth rose quickly up to the floor above. As soon as the booth was out of sight, the hatchway slammed closed.

"Karnowski says we foiled their plans! They still have great escape!"

"That Sheila is a remarkable woman." The Baron shook his head in admiration. "She would make a wonderful bride."

Lenny shook his head. The immediate threat was gone. "It's good to see you guys again."

Lenore looked him straight in the eye. He noticed how her hand brushed lightly against his elbow

"We never expected to be separated for so long," she said softly. He thought again of Lenore's reaction to Sheila. Was Lenore simply protecting a team member? Or could it be more than that?

"Karnowski knew Lenny would survive."

"But it was bad planning," Lenore continued with a frown. "Withers was more than just a werevole. He was our tactician as well."

For an instant, Lenny hoped that he might take over for Withers. Lenny could become a real part of the team—and maybe something more. But how could he possibly plan if he had no idea what his gift would bring him next?

"Wait!" the Baron shouted. "My creatures tell me we are not alone."

Lenny heard a scuffle coming from behind the fortune-telling machine. Many high-pitched rodent sounds mixed with someone crying, "Ow!" And "Get off me!" And "All right! I'll show myself!"

Lenny looked at the fortune-teller's turban and saw double. The owner of the second turban stepped out from his hiding place behind the glassed-in mannequin.

"Swami Phil!" Karnowski cried.

Phil bowed slightly in greeting. "I am still here. It was my choice to remain. And why was I hiding?" He looked at Lenny. "Because of Mr. Hodge. I was simply trying to determine the best way to approach your team." He pulled a struggling gray and furry mouse from inside his Nehru jacket. "Being driven from my hiding place by rats was not my first choice."

"My children!" the Baron called as the swami tossed the rat aside. The vampire looked to the others. "How can we trust a minion of Foo?"

But the Baron's objection did not faze Swami Phil. He continued to wear the same gentle smile as he continued his explanation.

"These last events have shown me something remarkable. Trying to take down someone with the sort of power Lenny Hodge holds would run counter to every rule in the Swami Code!"

It was Lenny's turn to ask the question. "The Swami Code?"

Phil nodded. "Certain rules all swamis wish to adhere to. What sort of rules? Rules against doing harm to old ladies, small children, and dogs. Rules about when you may swami for profit, and when you must do it for honor. And the greatest rule of all: that you must always help when you discover a magic greater than your own."

He looked straight at Lenny once more.

"I am done with Foo. I pledge to find the greater Lenny."

The ghost finder's frown deepened even more than usual. "Karnowski not so quick to trust!"

Lenore frowned in concentration. "I sense he is telling the truth—or believes he is telling the truth. He holds no falsehoods."

That was good enough for Lenny. Even when Phil was working for Foo, Lenny had thought the swami was kind of neat. "So let's hear what he's got planned. Swami, how can you help Terrifitemps?"

Phil glanced at their surroundings. "The first part of any plan is to get out of this place. Foo may be gone, but the treachery of this place remains."

Lenny waved at the collapsed wall where the buffalo had sung mere moments before. "Maybe we have a new exit."

The nameless ghost popped back into the room. "I've been exploring back there. Fine for someone made of ectoplasm. For someone who has to physically, uh, place your feet down on top of things, not such a good idea." He turned to look at the space behind the collapsed wall. "These bison sure could sing, but they also did"—the ghost paused, searching for just the right words—"what large animals do."

Lenny cautiously stepped forward and stuck his head through the large hole. The smell hit him before the sight. Whatever this space had been before, it was covered in plaster dust. But the plaster dust was covered as well, by large mounds of brown. The buffalo were gone, but they had left a part of themselves behind.

Lenore studied the odoriferous evidence from a distance. "So besides the fact that they were excellent choral singers, these buffalo were just—buffalo?"

"Yep," Lenny agreed. With Lenny, everything was always real. While that "everything" was also highly unlikely, it was entirely in the here and now; those were real singing bison, odiferous brown mounds included.

Swami Phil shook his head in admiration. "So your visitors are never more fantastic than they absolutely need to be. To actually see your gift in action—well." He whistled softly. "This is enough to get me Swami of the Year."

"You won't be swami of anything," the Baron reminded him crossly, "if we don't find a way out of here."

"But what about—that?" Lenny glanced back at the void, still whimpering in the corner. "Bob's still in there somewhere, isn't he? Should we try to get him out?"

Lenore shook her head. "One thing I've learned in all my years with

Terrifitemps. You never lose Bob the horse."

"We might lose ourselves if we don't start moving," the Baron grumbled.

"Exactly," Phil agreed. "I think we go out the way we came in." The swami led them out of the game room and into the hall. "With one quick detour," Phil added. He opened a door a few feet down the hall and went down a short set of stairs. The Terrifitemps team followed, with Lenny in the lead. He followed the swami through a second door that led into another large open space. Lenny couldn't see any people in this room, either. He saw a lot of tables, instead.

"This is Foo's central cafeteria," the swami said. "Most of Foo's lesser minions get lunch in here every day."

Lenny looked past the tables at half a dozen different food stations, advertising salads, pizza, sandwiches, and various hot meals. Lenny couldn't remember the last time he'd eaten something. His stomach growled in agreement.

"How can we tell food not booby-trapped?" Karnowski demanded.

"Food was very important to Foo. It may be the only place we won't find treachery." Phil waved to a food station just past the salad bar. "The road ahead will be difficult. I suggest that we all make sandwiches." He walked toward a station stocked with loaves of bread and luncheon meat.

The swami pointed to the stations on either side. "Other food is available. The stew is over there. Foo even stores supplies for those with specialized diets." He opened a silver door immediately beneath the sandwich counter. Inside hung three rows of dark-brown bags.

"Blood?" the Baron asked with a surprised smile. "Why would Foo keep blood on hand?"

"Do you think yours is the only organization to employ vampires?" Phil replied.

"Good point." The Baron bent over to get a closer look at the bags. "A-positive? My favorite type."

"We are still not alone," Karnowski said quietly. "Look over there."

Two shadowy figures lurked behind the soup station. They walked side by side toward Lenny. Their shadows walked with them.

"Please pardon our intrusion," one of them said, "and note that we have no immediate abduction plans for Mr. Hodge."

"While we hate to interrupt your meal," the other added, "we have to ask. What have you done with our supervisor?"

"The one you abandoned in the game room?" Lenore waved back at the entrance. "We haven't taken him anywhere."

The swirling void had reached the door to the cafeteria. It lurched inside, rolling erratically first one way and then another until it bumped against one of the many tables, where it partially absorbed an orange-plastic and metal chair. Lenny took a couple of careful steps toward the quivering darkness. The void was no longer groaning. Instead, Lenny thought he heard a constant, low-level sobbing. Beneath that blanket of misery, Lenny could hear another, fainter voice, muffled but cheerful, which was talking continuously, without even a pause for breath.

"Bob's still in there." Lenny knew no one else who could talk nonstop.

"He is?" one of the shadowy Dimm asked in alarm. "Oh dear. That changes everything."

"Maybe we don't need our supervisor back quite yet," the other Dimm agreed.

The two shadow figures began to slowly back away.

"You'll have to excuse us, Mr. Hodge. I'm afraid we'll have to threaten you some other time."

"We'll be waiting back in the game room. Just in case our supervisor regains his wits. Without Bob."

"Definitely without Bob."

A third of the lights went out overhead as the Dimm faded from the room.

Phil looked to the ceiling. "Foo's minions are still at work. Someone is shutting down the headquarters."

"Not to worry," the Baron replied. "We have ways of seeing in the dark."

"I'm not worried so much about the lights going out," Phil agreed. "It's what Foo has planned after the lights are gone that concerns me."

The lightless void dragged the half-absorbed chair as it struggled toward the edge of the room, rolling into a plastic trash can. It enveloped part of a plastic garbage can as it jerked forward. Its sobs were punctured by the occasional scream.

"I'm a little worried about Bob," Lenny admitted.

"Listen!" Karnowski added. "His problems rise to surface."

"I cannot bear another minute!" the void whimpered. "I don't want to hear one more word about the pooka polo team!"

"Okay!" Bob's voice, faint bur cheerful, replied. "What about a story about the pooka poker club? Or the pooka polka troupe?"

"No! No! No!" the darkness moaned. "I will self-destruct if I hear another word!"

"Oh." Bob sounded slightly taken aback. "If you felt that way about it, why didn't you just say so? I'll be leaving, then."

"Out!" the grand Dimm moaned. "Out!"

"But you know," Bob replied, "I never did finish my story about how pookas learned to perfect their pook—"

The void began to shriek.

"Could you stop screaming for just a minute?" Lenny could barely hear Bob's voice beneath the earsplitting void. "Which way is the door?"

"I fear Lenny may be correct in his concern," Bob said. "Who knows what will happen to a creature like the Dimm if he loses all sense of reason?"

"But Bob always lands on his feet," Lenore protested.

The lightless void began rolling back and forth, screaming ever louder. The chair and garbage can it dragged at its edges were joined by a half-enveloped table. The shrieks had grown so loud, Lenny could no longer hear Bob at all.

"Until now," Lenore admitted.

"And Bob did save me from this thing," Lenny added. "I think we should save him, too."

"Very well," the swami said with a nod. "I will once again summon the pooka."

Another bank of lights shut off overhead.

"Karnowski says we need to hurry!"

Phil nodded again. "I'll go as fast as I can. Would you give me a little room here? I have to do the cha-cha."

Sixteen

Lenny and the others moved a couple tables out of the way to allow Swami Phil some room to dance.

"One, two, one-two-three!" the swami chanted tonelessly. "One, two, one-two-three."

The darkness that was the Dimm grew very still. Lenny swore he could hear faint music coming from somewhere.

"One, two, one-two-three."

The void began to vibrate to the beat. The roiling darkness did not seem to enjoy the tune. The rhythmic grunts seemed more like complaints as it jerked about, dragging the cafeteria furniture in its wake.

Lenny thought he heard the faintest of whinnies.

"Yes!" Phil shouted and began to clap in time with the dance, his feet tracing intricate patterns on the cafeteria floor.

"Wait a moment!" an incredibly cheerful voice replied. "Do I see daylight?"

Lenny would know that annoying tone anywhere.

"Nobody can do boogaloo like I do, nobody can do shing-a-ling—wait, I'm out?" A ghostly blue figure materialized midair. He turned back to the still-pulsating void. "Anyways, as I was saying—that's why pookas seldom form glee clubs."

The void shrank away from the very mention of glee.

Only then did Bob seem to notice the rest of the Terrifitemps team. "Hey guys! Long time no talk!"

Lenny was the only one to say "hi" back.

The void expanded, then contracted with the slightest of quivers, as if taking a deep, ragged breath. Beyond that, the roiling darkness remained silent.

Bob grinned at everybody. "So you pulled me out? You must really be in trouble now!"

"I asked them to do it," Lenny answered for everyone. "We have to get out of here, and I didn't want to leave you behind."

"What?" Bob's smile turned down ever so slightly. "But we were having a fine time in there. I bet this Dimm guy never knew how educational I could be."

The void moaned softly. "Perfectly fine," it said in a voice just barely loud enough to be heard. "I'm sure we could talk some other time."

"I never got the chance to tell him how pookas invented opera," Bob continued. "Or how important they were to the development of woodworking. Let me back in there!"

The darkness jerked back violently, dragging the attached cafeteria furniture clattering behind it.

"No, Bob," Lenny insisted. "We have a bigger job to do. We have to save our co-workers at Terrifitemps, and make the world a safer place for all of us—pookas, too."

Bob paused. "Well, when you put it that way . . ."

"It's perfectly understandable if you have to leave," the void added tentatively. "Why don't you just go on your way? And take Bob with you. I'm all right with that. I'll peacefully live out the rest of my days, trapped by cafeteria furniture, but surrounded by peace and quiet."

Lenny decided they should take Bob and get out of here. He turned to say that to his team, and saw someone new blocking the door.

"What have you done to our supervisor?" one of two shadowy figures demanded.

"It wasn't us," Lenore told them flatly. "It was Bob."

The two shadows took a step away. "Bob's here?"

"And he's leaving!" the void called from behind the Terrifitemp team. "As long as you don't block his way. Why don't you come back later? In a day or two? I don't care. Now that I'm free of Bob, I'm reorganizing my priorities."

The void's shadowy subordinates looked to each other, conversing briefly in low tones. They both turned back toward Lenny and the team.

"O Fearless Leader," one of the two asked, "you mean you've given up your quest for world domination?"

"What's that?" the void replied tentatively. "World domination? No, I haven't given up. Let's say I don't quite see the need to go rushing into things." The darkness sighed. "Let me just stay in the cafeteria and smell the donuts. I think they're on that table over there."

The other Dimm still did not move. The void quivered in the corner. Everyone stood and stared at everyone else.

"I think this is a good time to leave," Lenny said to his team.

Karnowski frowned, waving at the swami in their midst. "We're taking this one with us?"

"He did give us Bob the horse," Lenny pointed out.

"And this is a point in his favor?" the Baron asked.

"Karnowski does not trust swamis."

"I remember that time you didn't like psychics," Lenore remarked.

"And the time you couldn't stand vampires," the Baron added. "And you should have heard what he thought about wervoles."

Karnowski bowed his head slightly. "Even ghost finders live and learn."

"Even the Dimm believe that discussion is sometimes in order," one of the two shadowy figures said from his spot by the entrance.

"But discussing would be much better on the other side of that door. After you've taken Bob with you."

"Once that is done," the first one added, "you will beware the power of the Dimm. Well, maybe not right away."

"But you'll probably feel our vengeance, eventually," the second one chimed in. "Just to let you know."

"You know," Bob mused, "these two could use a good talking to."

"Yes!" the void called from the back of the room. "You two talk to him!"

"No," Lenny replied. "We have places we need to be."

Bob considered this. "I really can't stop and talk to these guys?" He snorted in understanding. "I can't just think of myself. I'm part of the Terrifitemps team."

"Okay Bob!" Lenny shouted. "That's the spirit!"

The rest of the Terrifitemps team did not look so cheerful. Lenny still made sure everyone got out to the hallway.

"Now we talk to the swami," Lenore insisted. She poked her index finger at Phil's Nehru jacket. "You're responsible for everything that happened at Terrifitemps. Especially what happened to Withers and Ms. S.!"

The swami grinned a bit sheepishly. "Only in part. Foo's plans are complex. But yes, I can reverse what has happened. The spells I used are fairly benign. Your friends may not be able to perform their usual functions, but they will not come to harm."

Lenore didn't seem impressed. "And why did you come over to our side? So you could—observe—Lenny?"

"Only one of many reasons," Phil replied. "Foo wasn't following his part of the agreement. He was being less a monomaniacal leader and more the indulgent father. When Sheila wanted you dead, how could he refuse?" He turned to look appraisingly at Lenny. "What happened between the two of you, anyway?"

Lenny hadn't thought their relationship was that bad. But then, looking at the rest of his dating history, what did he have to compare it to?

"With Foo changing all the rules, how could I be true to the Swami Code?" Phil continued. "But I can tell you all about that later. Right now, my Swami Sense is telling me it's time we leave."

"Not so fast!" Foo's voice boomed from far overhead. "I'm not through with you yet!"

"And neither am I," Sheila's voice came from behind them. Lenny spun around to see her marching in their direction. She had changed from her black evening dress into a more sensible V-neck sweater and jeans. She had pulled her short long blonde hair into a stubby ponytail. And she was frowning. This looked like the Sheila he remembered.

"You're not leaving," she continued, in a voice that said she expected to be obeyed. "It's high time we finished this. We're going to have the talk we needed to have so long ago. Or else."

Lenny realized she was carrying a revolver in her right hand.

"That talk?" he whispered, mostly to himself. What did that mean? And did the talking involve guns?

"Wow," Bob the horse said softly at Lenny's side. "She even scares me."

Seventeen

"You would be wise not to move!" the voice boomed over the intercom. "We have you surrounded."

Sheila stopped to look distractedly at the ceiling.

"Oh, Daddy," she murmured. "Always with the big talk."

"What are you saying?" Karnowski demanded. "He doesn't have us surrounded?"

Sheila frowned and shook her head. "He's still far too disorganized to do much of anything. As long as his secret plans stay secret, he's fine. As soon as he gets any interference—you guys showing up, the swami defecting, pretty much anything that's happened to Lenny—he falls apart."

"You'll rue the day you crossed Foo!"

"He's just trying to confuse you until he comes up with a something he really can do," Sheila continued. "Since one of his former planners is now with you, it makes it that much more difficult."

"Lose all hope, pitiful mortals!" Maniacal laughter boomed from overhead.

Every pronouncement from Foo seemed to make Sheila more annoyed. "You're safe for now. As long as he's talking, he's not doing."

Lenny wasn't sure he should believe her. "Then why is he laughing?"

"He just likes to show off his state-of-the-art sound system. You know how men are." She pointed an accusing finger. "You, Lenny Hodge, of all people, know that."

Lenny's mind was racing. He knew how men were what?

"Laugh has very good bass and treble," Karnowski said. "But we believe this woman—why?"

Lenore frowned in Sheila's direction. "I have some difficulty seeing her true intentions. Mostly she seems—conflicted."

Conflicted? Lenny didn't think that sounded at all promising.

"Or maybe she's—confused," Lenore added. Her frown deepened. "Or confessional. Or maybe confounded. Confuscatory?"

"The outlook is hazy," the swami agreed. He looked pointedly at Sheila. "We would all feel better if you put that gun away."

"Oh, this?" Sheila looked at the gun as if it had jumped into her hand. "These are all over the place. I sometimes forget I'm carrying one."

"Now she's lying," Lenore said in a much more certain tone.

Sheila stared at the other woman.

"You're right. I do feel like shooting someone. But who?"

"I will finally defeat Terrifitemps!" the voice crowed overhead. "No one can stand in my way."

"We'll just ignore that," Sheila continued. "I do seem to have this gun." She surveyed the Terrifitemps team. "It would be a shame not to use it."

She looked at Lenny first. "Oh Lenny." She sighed. "Bottom line—I still haven't worked out my feelings."

"Everybody loves Lenny!" Bob the horse agreed.

Sheila looked fondly at the gun in her hands. "Lenny, you're working for the enemy. Why can't I just get over you and put a bullet through your heart?"

The gun waved to Lenny's left.

"Or what about the traitor in our midst?" Sheila asked.

Phil shook his head. "The swami way is the way of peace. Well, peace and profit. Or peace, profit, and continuing curiosity. Don't you want to know what makes Lenny tick?"

"I tried," Sheila replied wearily. "I really tried."

"Everybody loves Lenny's ticks!" Bob the horse added.

The gun moved past Phil to point at Lenore. "Or maybe I'll just shoot my romantic rival. If I can't have Lenny, then nobody can."

What? Lenny and Lenore had only met a few hours ago. He glanced at his redheaded teammate. She was certainly attractive, if maybe a little spooky. But romance? No matter what Lenny might hope for at some quiet time in the future, right now they were all too busy with crazed criminal masterminds, not to mention their equally crazed gun-toting daughters.

"You're talking nonsense," Lenore replied. "You're confusing him. Let it go. That Lenny Hodge is a person out of the past. He's moved beyond you now."

"He has, has he?" Sheila was shouting now. She moved closer, waving her gun back and forth between Lenore and Lenny. "Hah! You'll never see your first day cover again."

Lenny blinked. Since he had joined Terrifitemps, he had hardly even thought about his stamp collection. As rare as that cover was, maybe it was the price he had to pay to have Sheila out of his life forever.

"You still try to escape, pitiful fools? It will do you no good. Wait! My daughter is—where?"

"Hi, Daddy." Sheila waved.

"How can I be the world's foremost criminal mastermind if my own daughter won't listen to me?"

Foo's daughter sighed and looked away.

"I was planning to destroy them with a wall of fire! But no, my own daughter is in my way!"

Sheila pointed her gun up toward the state-of-the-art speakers. "I may have some issues with you, Lenny, but my father can be really difficult."

"I think Sheila needs a good lesson. What if I flood the whole complex while you're standing—"

Everybody jumped as Sheila pulled the trigger, sending a bullet into the ceiling.

"Quite an echo in here," the Baron remarked as the loud bang reverberated down the hall. Lenny noticed that the Baron was inching away from the others in his party. Bullets didn't kill vampires, did they? Maybe he was trying to distract Sheila. But to what end?

"You are limiting yourself, my dear," the Baron continued. He had moved to the far side of the hall, a few yards distant from the other Terrifitempers, and had begun to glide in Sheila's direction. "Why settle for a short and unhappy life with the likes of Lenny when you could spend the rest of eternity as a vampire bride?"

"Another one?" Karnowski asked. "Karnowski thought you reached your limit—at least one bride ago."

"I have no limits," the vampire admitted. "Not when I meet someone as feisty as this."

"My mother had a thing for vampires." Sheila made a face. "Me, not so much."

Lenny wondered if feisty and crazy could be synonyms. He frowned. Did he see movement out of the corner of his eye?

"Nobody ever asks the pooka," Bob interjected petulantly.

Sheila frowned at the ghostly blue horse. "Ask what?"

"For the secrets you hide even from yourself within your heart," Bob replied wistfully. "Pookas are the masters of romance."

"That's it!" Sheila screamed. "I may have to shut up and listen to my father, but the day I take advice from a horse—"

Lenny winced as Sheila fired off three quick shots in Bob's direction.

Bob whinnied as the bullets passed through him to ricochet farther down the hall.

"That tickles. But as I was saying—"

Lenny saw movement on either side of the hall, two lines of flowing black, like water rushing ahead of an approaching flood, both lines heading straight for Sheila.

The Baron's cape rustled as he threw up his arms. "Now, my children! Make your master proud!"

The two lines at the corridor's edges fanned out, rushing Sheila from either side. Lenny realized the moving darkness was hundreds, maybe thousands, of cockroaches, swirling around his ex-girlfriend, climbing up both in and out of her clothes to her waist, her arms, heading toward her face.

"Ick! Ack!" Sheila screamed. "Ewww!" She shot at the floor a couple times, but the roaches were not deterred. They swept up and over her like a great, crawling tide.

"No! You can't!" Sheila continued. But then she spoke no more, for the insects had reached her chin and were close to crawling into her mouth. She made a gagging noise, dropped her gun, and ran. She fled down the hall, shedding roaches behind her.

The discarded insects swirled in her wake, forming letters as they spread across the floor. The Baron read the words aloud with pride.

this pretty woman
should not carry a weapon
if we can help it

He beamed as he looked back to the rest of his team. "Such talented insects."

Sheila's shrieks faded with distance. Somewhere, in some other faraway hallway, Foo was shouting out of some other intercom, too far away for Lenny to make out the words.

"Karnowski astonished we have moment's peace."

Swami Phil nodded. "You seem to have temporarily pushed back the legions of Foo. We may even have time for a counterattack."

"A counterattack?" Lenore asked. "We've already thrown ghosts and roaches at them. What do we have left?"

"They even laugh at the power of the pooka!" Bob agreed.

"We still have the greatest weapon of all." The swami paused for a minute to roll back the sleeves of his Nehru jacket. "Lenny, you are about to reach your full potential."

Eighteen

"Where are we—exactly?" the swami mused.

"In reaching Lenny's full potential?" Lenore asked.

"No, where are we in Foo's secret headquarters? We need someplace a little out of the way if we're to give ourselves enough time to make this succeed."

He walked over to the wall on the left-hand side of the corridor. "I believe we have a minute to reconnoiter. After that, it's best if we are hidden from the hallway cameras."

Swami Phil took a moment to look up and down the hallway. He moved two steps to his right, then knocked on the wall, sharply, three times, midway between floor and ceiling.

Lenny heard a faint whirring sound. A panel slid away on the wall in front of the swami, revealing a large video screen. Lenny and the rest of the team crowded in behind Phil. The screen displayed a map of one part of the headquarters, complete with a large red X and the words "You are here."

"Just what we needed," Phil said to himself. "Now where do we go from here? What else is on this level?" Phil touched his finger to the display and began to move it slowly to the right. The swami traced his finger down the corridor on the screen, and the map display began to move as well.

"The airplane hangar?" he mused before shaking his head. "Too obvious a means of escape." The finger traveled a few inches farther. "The satellite library? No, they'll expect us to seek out information."

His finger moved farther along the map. "There will be people around the barber shop and the bowling alley." He paused. "We might be able to subdue the clerk in the flower shop, but it's right beside the gift kiosk."

"Aha!" Phil slapped the screen with the palm of his hand. He turned to the others and smiled. "We're going to the comedy club."

The swami abruptly turned left and walked down the hall. After an instant's hesitation, the rest of the team followed. They pursued Phil around the corner into a new hallway with a dozen different doors on either side. The swami opened the third door on the left.

"Foo always operates according to a grand vision," Phil said as the others followed him into the room.

"He was intent on building a full-service secret headquarters," Phil explained. "But some services were never completed. This particular project was doomed to fail."

Lenny looked around the large room, walls and curtains done all in shades of deep red. He saw a bar on the far side of the room. The shelves behind the bar were empty. Chairs were stacked atop half a dozen dime-sized circular tables.

Lenny felt somebody had to ask. "Why would a comedy club fail?"

"Foo doesn't find anything funny," Phil replied.

"What's with creepy laughter, then?" Karnowski asked.

"Well, except maybe total world domination," Phil admitted. "But that's not exactly comedy club material."

The swami walked over to the raised stage at the far end of the room. "This room is a nice open space. Almost totally forgotten, until Foo decides to remodel it into another chamber of doom or some such."

Phil turned to face the others. "It is perfect for what we need to do next. I need quiet. And I'll need Lenny to concentrate."

"So Lenny will be at your mercy, then?" Karnowski demanded. "You claim to be on our side now, but what happens when Lenny is in your power?"

"I sense no ill will," Lenore said with her customary frown of concentration. "The need for advancement, the desire to make a quick buck, a burning urge to one day make infomercials. But no ill will."

"We are on the edge of a great new frontier." The swami slapped Lenny's back. "We will plumb the true depths of Lenny's abilities. Where do they come from, where do they lead? What are Lenny's true capabilities?" He turned back to the rest of the team. "Ladies and gentlemen, prepare to enter the Lennyverse."

Even the Baron frowned at that. "That sounds vast—and dangerous."

Swami Phil shook his head, a smile of inspiration on his lips. "Look at what we have witnessed so far. I think, whatever threatens Lenny, and I mean really threatens him, his gift will save him from the threat."

Even Lenore seemed skeptical of that. "And we can depend on that—why?"

"Because I won't be doing the driving—Lenny will. I am going to attempt to put that gift under Lenny's direct control. But come, we must begin. Even here, we risk the chance of discovery. Lenny, if you will step on stage?"

Lenny did as he was told.

"Now, if you will look at me?" Swami Phil unbuttoned the top of his Nehru jacket and reached within to pull out a number of medallions, each attached to a gold or silver chain around the swami's neck.

"Wow!" Bob the horse whistled. "That's a lot of bling!"

Phil nodded. "Even my mystical powers will not get me through airport security." He turned to look at Lenore. "I will need your help. We must determine which amulet is the most appropriate. All of these have positive qualities. But which is best for our current purpose?"

Lenore frowned in concentration as Phil lifted each pendant in turn. The first was a simple silver oval.

"I will describe each amulet's primary power—as I have perceived them. But some of these mystic ornaments may have further uses far beyond what I have discovered. This first object is particularly useful for reaching out to deceased relatives in the vast beyond."

Lenore nodded at his description. Phil moved on to the next chain, and what looked like a jagged piece of petrified wood. "This one will help you to find water in the desert."

The third pendant showed two large silver letters "SP" encrusted with small, glittering stones. "This one helps you make better rhymes with a hip-hop beat." Next, he fingered a golden amulet, studded with emeralds and rubies. "And this particular piece is great for starting conversations with single women in bars."

Lenore's frown, if anything, was deeper than before. "Each is as the swami has stated. Were we looking for water or hoping to pick up girls?" Lenore sighed. "I can think of nothing in the least bit useful here."

"Pookas are always useful!" Bob piped up from the back of the crowd.

Phil sighed as he studied the four medallions he held in his hands. "On reflection, these are not quite as powerful as I had hoped. I must pull out the final amulet, the one I use in emergencies."

He let the first four pendants bounce against his chest as he reached inside his jacket one more time. This final chain sported a gem larger than any of the medallions Lenny had seen before. The huge stone sparkled even in the club's indirect lighting.

"Impressive!" the Baron remarked. "Is that a diamond?"

"Actually," Phil replied, "it's a cubic zirconia, but by far the finest zirconia that can be produced today." He twirled the chain between his fingers. "It is an artificial gem of awesome power."

"Lenore?" Karnowski demanded. "Does swami finally speak true?"

The young woman took a step away from the glittering stone.

"This is almost beyond my comprehension." She shook her head. "Something within this zirconia can reflect and redirect forces of tremendous—almost unbelievable—completely off the scale—" She took a deep breath. "All I can say is wow!"

Swami Phil nodded as if he expected no less. "Then we shall begin. We need quiet, and something more. We will be dealing with the ghosts of Lenny's past. And ghosts respond best to other ghosts." He waved toward the back of the room. "Perhaps we might find a real ghost among our number."

"Me?" a tremulous voice responded from the edge of the crowd.

"The nameless ghost?" the Baron asked. "I had forgotten he was here."

"I get that a lot," the ghost agreed, real excitement in its voice. "Who knew I'd go from that boring pit into a life of adventure?"

"Are you sure," Lenore asked, "as eager as he is, that this ghost is the right one for the job?"

"I can think of other volunteers!" Bob the horse agreed.

Karnowski waved away the pooka's objection. "It must be. Foo installed too many protections. This structure and this room filled with strong wards that prevent me from summoning any further spirits. Besides, if Karnowski knows his ghosts, our friend here will be perfect guide."

"Very good." The swami turned back to the small raised stage. "Lenny. Are you ready?'

Lenny nodded. He was more than ready. The swami was going to open Lenny's past. Would it bring him a greater understanding of his gift? Maybe even the true meaning of his life? For the first time since he could remember, Lenny felt genuinely excited.

"I need you to concentrate. We must prepare to send you into a trance"—Phil clapped his hands three times—"swami style!"

The swami swung the jewel casually back and forth. "First, a ground rule or two. You are returning to your past, but it is a remembered past, a past that is dynamic, even capable of change. This is about exploring your gift. Whatever happens, do not become mired in the days that you have left behind.

"If you feel trapped, frustrated, held back, you must only snap your fingers to move ahead. Snap your fingers, and the gift will come."

"Snap my fingers?" Lenny asked as his eyes followed the zirconia.

"Like this." Phil rubbed thumb and index finger together with an audible snap.

Lenny looked down at his right hand. He was never very good at snapping his fingers.

"Go ahead," Phil urged. "Try it."

This time, his fingers snapped just fine. Maybe this trance thing was working already. Lenny smiled. He snapped his fingers again. Did he imagine it, or did the air shimmer around him?

"Very good." Phil returned to twirling the pendant before him. "And one more thing. Even with all our safeguards, this trance can lead to danger. We will need a safe word, in case we find some negative aspects of your power, or your gift takes you too far; a word that when spoken will return you to the here and now. It should be but a single word. Something not casually used, but easy to remember."

Word? Lenny thought as the gem sparkled before him. Maybe he could come up with something after he took a little nap.

Phil nodded to Lenny's right. "Is our guide prepared?"

"I am ready to do my ghostly duty!"

The zirconia spun.

"You're letting that ghost do this?" Bob complained loudly. "When you have a pooka right here? I say thee nay!"

The swami looked at Bob for a long moment.

"The safe word is onomatopoeia," he said at last.

"That sounds like the mambo!" Bob the horse enthused. "Onomatopoeia! Onomatopoeia!" The pooka swung his ghostly blue hips to the rhythm.

The gem swung and shone.

"I am beginning to regret my cha-cha exorcism spell," Phil admitted. "Anyway, once you have heard this word you will be awake and fully restored, as if you had just woken from a healthy nap."

"Onomatopoeia!" Bob sang. "Onomato-pee-a!"

"Onomatopoeia?" Lenny repeated.

Lenny was suddenly awake. He was in the middle of a big, red room, with the rest of Terrifitemps staring at him. And Swami Phil had been explaining—what?

"Huh?" Lenny asked. "What am I doing?"

Phil grabbed the twirling gem in his right hand and turned to glare at the pooka. "Bob, please! This spell is of utmost importance. Lenny's very existence may be at stake!"

"Very existence?" Bob crossed his front forelegs and bowed his head. "I suppose I wouldn't want to do that. Is it my fault that pookas were born to dance?"

"Now, everyone, calm and quiet please." The swami turned back to the dais. "Remember, Lenny. You should only use your safe word as a last resort."

The zirconia sparkled.

"Now stare into the gem."

Lenny did as he was told. The large cubic zirconia spun before him. Who cared about safe words? It was calm in there with the sparkling lights.

"Oogleybook," Phil intoned in a low but powerful voice. "Nanglytoot, chim chim cheree. Wampun, stompun, goolyflaspmun. You are in my power."

Goolyflaspmun? Lenny thought absently. But the world around him was drifting away.

"I am in your power," he said aloud.

"Exactly. Now relax, and let the ghost be your guide."

The gem sparkled.

Lenny relaxed, and drifted.

"You seek an earlier time," the swami continued. "A simpler time. Go back, back, back."

"Earlier time," the ghost's voice echoed. "Simpler. Back, back, back."

Lenny took a deep breath and opened his eyes.

Nineteen

Sheila was asleep on the pillow next to him.

She looked different. Younger, more innocent perhaps. He remembered that Sheila well, back when they had first been together. Now, he was back next to her again.

He remembered just how he had felt about her. His first true love. And he remembered what happened after that, and how that pure and wonderful feeling was a thing from his past.

He lifted his own head from his pillow. The bedroom beyond Sheila was hazy, indistinct, as if obscured by mist. Lenny heard something droning in his ear. Sheila was still asleep. But somebody else was talking, growing louder with every word.

"I am the ghost of Lenny past!" a voice announced from somewhere close by. "Here to show you past errors, and the possibility of redemption. Here to reveal a pivotal day, the importance of which you only now may see."

Lenny studied the young woman sleeping at his side. Things had seemed so simple then. When he and Sheila were first together, the world was bright and new.

Sheila opened her eyes and smiled. "Wow. I knew you were special. But not that special."

Lenny blinked. Everything about the night before came flooding back in surprising detail. It felt like hours ago rather than years, no doubt some further benefit of the swami's spell.

Lenny smiled. He had known (way back then) the night before was pretty good, but he never imagined how good. Multiple times good. It seemed quite remarkable from a couple of years farther down the line. He had definitely been inspired.

Sheila pushed up against him. His hand brushed against her stomach. She was naked under the sheet.

She leaned close to his ear to whisper. "Why don't we pick up where we left off?"

He was surprised how ready he was to take her up on that. But that wasn't what he was here for—was it? Lenny thought briefly about what his body was asking him to do. Well, why not? How could he really know what he was here for until he tried—everything?

"Be aware of all your senses!" the ghost announced in his other ear. Lenny yelped.

"Are my hands cold?" Sheila asked.

"No, it's not that," Lenny assured her.

"Your gift is here," the ghost continued. "Look, and listen!"

How could Lenny do anything with constant ghostly interruptions?

He smiled at Sheila. "I guess I'd just like to talk."

Sheila smiled at that as well. How long had it been since he had made Sheila really smile? Today he could do no wrong.

"Okay. There's lots to talk about." Sheila sighed in contentment. "We have our whole lives together."

If only she knew. What had led both of them to their lives together, their lives apart, and finally to their meeting in Foo's secret headquarters? If Swami Phil was correct, it began right here.

"Seek the answers you must find!" the ghost cheered.

Lenny shook his head. "I don't know how to find what I'm looking for."

"We're both young. We don't need to have all the answers." Sheila squeezed his arm. "I don't think you put enough faith in yourself. You're somebody who can do great things. Together, we could do just about anything."

He turned and looked at Sheila's bright blue eyes. He had felt that way about both of them, once.

Sheila's breast brushed against his elbow. "Remember what you did last night, with your tongue?"

Even he had to admit that was pretty remarkable. Maybe he could delay his quest for answers just a little while.

"Sheila holds the clue!"

Lenny started as the ghost barked in his ear.

Sheila pulled back from his side to frown up at him. "Are you okay?"

"Yeah," he replied. Except I have a ghost shouting in my ear. He glanced back at Sheila. How could Lenny explain the unexplainable?

He decided he couldn't. "Maybe I should go to the bathroom."

"Good idea. I'll try to scare up some breakfast while you're gone."

Sheila climbed out of bed and walked, naked, into the kitchen. Lenny did his best to look the other way. He had to concentrate. Who knew how long this spell would last? He had a mission, to find the true meaning of his gift. He left the bedroom and turned into the bathroom, closing the door behind him.

"Ghost?" he asked when he was done peeing. "I appreciate your assistance, but could you not shout in my ear?"

"The swami told me it was important to cheer you on, keep you focused!" the ghost insisted.

"I understand that! But I'd like not to jump every time you say something!"

The ghost thought otherwise. "This is the most important job I've had in eons! It could be a turning point in my ghostly existence. What if we really find the true nature of your gift? And I really helped? Nobody would forget—well, whatever my name is—then!"

Lenny sighed. "All right. Give me pointers when you think I need them, but from here on in, you need to let me lead the way."

"Swami Phil says I can't let you get distracted." The ghost was getting even more excited. "I need to urge you ever onward to your goal!"

"Could you just do it a bit more quietly?" Lenny realized he was shouting as well.

"Are you talking to me, sweetie?" Sheila called from the other side of the bathroom door.

"We'll discuss this later," Lenny hissed in a tense whisper. He turned toward the door, but turned back for an instant. Sheila didn't like it when he didn't put the toilet seat back down.

He opened the bathroom door and walked down the short hall to the kitchen. He was relieved to see that Sheila had put on his old terry-cloth robe. He needed to get past any distractions and find out why he was really here.

"Sorry," he said as he walked into the room. "Just talking to myself."

"Why don't you come over here and I can talk back at you?" She held out a steaming mug. "I made you some coffee. Beyond that, your pantry is bare." She lifted a cereal box and shook it. It sounded almost empty. "You've got a little raisin bran. No milk." She put down the box and picked up a paper-wrapped pastry, which she then rapped against the counter. The pastry knocked with a solid clunk. "And I think these Pop-Tarts are prehistoric."

Lenny started to apologize.

"Hush, lover," Sheila interrupted before he could say any more. "This just proves how much you need me around. You need a good woman in your life. Maybe it's time I moved in."

Sheila moving in? That had been the beginning of the end for their relationship. When this had first happened, really happened, he had been surprised and flattered. And, more importantly, he hadn't said no. The second time around, he wondered if he could change the outcome.

"I'd really like that, but what would you do with your apartment?" he countered.

"Let me worry about that." Sheila replied. "My father knows the landlord."

"Well, let's talk about it, then," Lenny countered.

"Isn't that what we're doing now?"

Lenny sighed. "But there are other things to consider, before you—I mean, before we—make any big life change." He could feel his voice grow quieter and less sure as he tried to explain. "If we really want to have a life together, if we want to make it work, shouldn't we talk about it first?"

Sheila frowned. Her angry frown. Lenny knew that frown. "I'm beginning to think that you don't want me around!"

Great. Instead of preventing a bad move that would affect both their futures, Lenny had managed to sink his relationship here and now. And why was he trying to change things, anyway? Shouldn't he just be reliving the moment here, looking for clues? After all that had happened, did he still have feelings for Sheila?

"Why don't you answer me?" Sheila demanded. "Am I just someone you want to take to bed and get rid of the following morning?"

"No, of course n—" Lenny began.

But Sheila was beyond listening to anything he said. "My mother warned me about men like you. I should have listened!"

"Pardon?" The ghost spoke much more softly in Lenny's ear.

"I'm in the middle of something here," Lenny whispered back. "What do you want?"

"You don't have to be in the middle," the ghost insisted. "The swami saw a way out of this."

The swami? Lenny did his best to tune out Sheila's continuing rant. What had Swami Phil said about controlling the situation? What the heck. It was worth a try.

"Are you even listening to me?" Sheila demanded.

Lenny snapped his fingers.

The anger drained from Sheila's face. "Oh?" she said with a smile. "Well, I'm glad that's settled."

It was? Lenny did his best to remain calm. Maybe they could get back to revisiting what actually happened, and Lenny could discover the secrets of his past.

"So what should we do today?" Sheila continued. "You promised to show me your stamp collection."

He had, hadn't he? Now he was getting back to the past he remembered. He seldom showed his stamps to anyone. This just proved how serious his feelings for Sheila had been.

"Do you want to look at them now?" he asked. "Aren't you hungry?"

Sheila stepped closer to him. "I'm more curious than hungry. Your stamps are so important to you. Why don't you tell me a little bit about them?" She gently rubbed his shoulder. "And then we can think of something else to do."

"Okay," Lenny agreed quickly. He had to concentrate, really concentrate, on what had actually happened. "I'll just show you a couple of my prizes." He walked over to the closet to retrieve the three-ring binders.

"Remember the stamps!" The ghost was shouting again.

"You were telling me about a first day cover?" Sheila said softly.

He supposed he must have. It was the most valuable part of his collection, the 1934 red-and-blue Moldavian Lindhberg stamp with the red ink inverted. Only seven of these first day covers were known to exist, the few the post office had sent out before they realized their error. And, at the age of eight, Lenny had found one.

"When did you first notice your gift?" the ghost whispered in his ear.

Lenny paused to think as he opened the closet door. The ghost asked an interesting question. He had no knowledge of his gift when he was really young. But later, sometime in grade school, small, odd things began to happen. He remembered trying to tell his mother about the singing frog he'd discovered. And the things that followed the frog. His mother alternately thought he had an overactive imagination or just wanted attention. After a while, she told him she didn't want to hear any more of his stories. His father just got angry and told him to pay more attention to his homework. So Lenny started keeping the strange happenings to himself. And, after a while, he sometimes thought they might be in his imagination as well.

Sheila had asked to see the first day cover. Remember the stamps! It was the same first day cover that Sheila had stolen two years later. And the same cover, the ghost suggested, that may have been the first of the many unlikely things that happened in his life.

"You're my lover! You're my lover!" A jaunty pop song erupted from Sheila's purse, where she had left it in the living room. Lenny recognized the song as one of the ringtones on Sheila's cell phone.

"Excuse me a second." She walked into the other room and retrieved her phone.

"Hello?" Sheila listened for a moment. "Oh, I totally forgot." She paused for a reply. "Well, I'm not at home." Another moment. "If you really feel it's necessary." She gave the caller the address of Lenny's building. "Fine. Pick me up out front in half an hour."

Sheila tossed her phone back in her purse. "I have to get dressed. That was my parents. We'll have to admire your stamps some other time."

This was altogether wrong. Sheila hadn't been talking to her parents back at the time she and Lenny were first together—or so she had said. She certainly never got a call from them at his apartment. At this point in the real past, hadn't he just shown her the stamps? She had oohed and ahhed over each one, maybe showing a bit more enthusiasm than she had felt. But Lenny had been in the throes of young love and could see no wrong.

Did this change mean something? Was his gift trying to tell him something even now?

"Don't worry," she called to Lenny over her shoulder. "I'll meet them downstairs." She went back into the bedroom to put her clothes on.

But he had to show her the stamps. His interaction with Sheila was the purpose of his being here.

"Do you really have to go?" he called.

"They need me," she said from the other room. "It's a family thing."

What would a Foo family gathering look like? Images popped into Lenny's head. Dividing up the spoils of their secret accounts? Getting together their plans for world domination? Lenny decided he didn't want to know. He felt like events were spiraling beyond his control. And this time, he didn't need his ghostly guide to tell him what to do.

Lenny snapped his fingers.

He was sitting next to Sheila on his couch, his stamp collection spread on the coffee table before him.

That's more like it, Lenny thought. He turned to Sheila.

"So what do you think?'

She smiled down at the open binders. "I can see why these are so important to you. The foreign stamps are beautiful."

She looked at Lenny. "Except I wonder about that one very valuable stamp."

"You mean the first day cover?" Lenny had hoped this would come up.

"How did you find that again?"

"It was stuck in the middle of a bundle of newspapers. Somebody had left them in the basement of our apartment building, right next to the trash cans. I needed some newspapers for a school project. I opened the bundle, and there it was."

"What incredible luck." Sheila smiled at him. "It just shows how lucky you are. Think of all the things you can do!"

Lenny paused. Sheila had probably said that before. Only now did Lenny even think about that phrase "the things you can do." Had Sheila known something about his gift way back then?

"But you say it's really valuable," Sheila said.

"Probably. It's very rare."

"Do you think it's safe sitting in your closet? What if someone were to come in and steal it?"

"Nobody knows about my stamp collection but me." His mother had known, but she had passed away a couple of years ago. He looked at Sheila. "And now you."

Sheila reached over and took Lenny's hand. "You've made me feel really special. I hope I never do anything do betray your trust."

Like stealing the first day cover a couple years from now? he didn't say aloud.

This seemed much the same way the conversation had happened, back in the real past. But did it say anything more about his gift?

Somebody banged on the door.

"Sheila!" a deep male voice called. "I know you're in there!"

The color drained from Sheila's face. "It's my father. How could he know I'm here?"

Maybe because she had spoken to him on the phone? But that was before Lenny had snapped his fingers. Lenny no longer had any idea of the cause and effect in this place. Foo was outside of Lenny's apartment? Maybe it was time to stop talking about stamps. The risk here seemed far worse than the reward.

"Onoma—" Lenny began.

"Shush!" Sheila put her hand over his mouth. "My father's very old school. If he hears I'm in here with a man, we could be in real trouble."

"Sheila! Open the door!"

What if he didn't use the safe word? Maybe this situation could still be salvaged.

Lenny snapped his fingers.

Foo kept on pounding. "Open this door at once!"

This whole changing the scenario thing seemed to be wearing out its welcome. Lenny looked around the room. Had his latest snap done anything?

"This looks like a job for a pooka!"

Sheila gasped as Bob popped into view in front of the door.

"Hi, Lenny!" Bob said.

"Wow." Sheila sounded truly impressed. "You know a ghostly blue horse? Lenny, you become more interesting with every passing minute."

Apparently, nothing fazed Sheila.

"I hear a man's voice in there!" Foo yelled through the door.

"Actually, it's a pooka!" Bob replied.

"I don't give a hoot about your nationality," Foo replied. "Get away from my daughter!"

"Don't come in that door," Bob shouted back, "or you will taste pooka vengeance!"

"I hear a man's voice making threats!" Foo shot back. "You leave me no choice, Sheila. I don't have to break the door down myself. I've brought my minions to do it for me!"

"Daddy!" Sheila shouted back. "You know how I feel about them. How can I have any private life at all if your minions keep getting in the way?"

Lenny shook his head. This made even less sense than what had happened before. Bob the horse here? Now?

"Why?" Lenny decided the direct approach was the best. "Bob? Why are you here?"

Bob grinned in his direction. "Swami Phil sensed you might be in trouble."

"And he sent you?"

"No, I came on my own. My pal Lenny needed me. It was time to show some pooka initiative!"

It's really time, Lenny thought, to get out of here.

"On—" Lenny began again.

The door burst open with a crash. Sheila screamed and fell against Lenny, throwing both of them to the floor.

"Mmm-mmm!" Lenny managed.

Sheila had fallen on top of him, her sweater pressed into his nose, making it impossible to breathe, much less talk.

"And what do you want?" he heard Bob demand.

"There's a horse in here?" Foo screamed. "They have defiled my daughter! Kill them all!"

"Onomatopoeia!" the nameless ghost shouted in response.

Everything went dark.

Twenty

"Are you all right?" a woman's gentle, concerned voice asked. "What happened?"

Lenny opened his eyes and looked up at Lenore. He smiled, safely out of the dream. But how could he answer that: What hadn't happened?

"All I know is I'm really happy to be back here. Things were getting a little hectic in my dream state." Swami Phil stepped close enough for Lenny to see him. "It was a dream state, right?"

Phil nodded curtly. "More or less. That's not the proper swami-certified mystical metaphysical technical term, but close enough."

Lenny propped himself up on his elbows—for some reason, he was lying flat on the stage—and tried to summarize what had happened as the Terrifitemps team gathered around him. No one interrupted until he started talking about the first day cover.

"That was what your gift was taking you to find," the swami said.

Lenny had thought the same thing. "My gift is all tied in with that first day cover, but how?"

"So, perhaps the first day cover is a catalyst for your gift," Lenore began.

"Karnowski thinks it could be first manifestation of gift."

The Baron stroked his right fang in thought. "Or it was some sort of coincidence, but it made you more aware of your surroundings so you could thus become aware of your gift."

Lenny considered all of that.

"Well, yeah. I guess so."

"So you learned something about that first day cover," Swami Phil prompted. "And what happened next?"

Lenny paused a moment before he replied. "Everything I saw seemed exactly the same as when it actually happened—which was about two years ago. Until suddenly things changed." Lenny nodded. "More and more, as my trance continued, events kept wandering away from how I remembered them.

"I snapped my fingers to bring things back on track. It seemed to work at first, but later it just made things stranger." He took a deep breath. "At one point, I asked a question that I hadn't asked in the past, and that seemed to accelerate the changes."

Lenny went on to discuss the stranger part.

"Interesting," Phil replied. "As your gift got more involved in your trance, the past changed with it."

"But I thought you said my gift would protect me," Lenny replied. "The second or third time I snapped my fingers, Foo showed up. I snapped my fingers again, and Foo was going to kill me!"

The swami stared at Lenny for an instant before asking, "Yet the gift brought you back here, didn't it?"

"Finally, though it was mostly thanks to my ghostly guide." Lenny looked at Lenore, and decided not to describe how Sheila had fallen on top of him. "He was the one who shouted the safe word."

Karnowski looked around the room.

"Where is ghost, anyway?"

A pitiful, spectral moan came from the far corner of the room.

Lenny sat up and watched the others rush toward the noise. He could see the nameless ghost, not all that substantial at the best of times, flickering in their midst.

The spirit's voice was barely more than a whisper. "Barely . . . made it back . . . one piece."

"Why can we hardly see him?" Lenore demanded.

The ghost murmured in reply. "Sorry . . . took it out of me . . . need rest."

"Ghosts can get exhausted?" the Baron demanded. "I have never heard of that before."

Karnowski seemed to take offense at that. "Ghosts are capable of many things. Flight, noise, chilling cold, half-heard songs, even exhaustion."

Swami Phil waved back at the stage of the comedy club. "All things are possible when we are in the presence of Lenny. Your gift transcends the boundaries of the spirit world."

Lenny pushed himself up and tried to walk toward the others. He was a little unsteady on his feet. He managed to sit at the edge of the stage to get a better view.

"Karnowski sees many strange ghosts, and many ghostly reactions. This ghost is at limits, but not beyond my experience." He studied the flickering form before him. "With rest, ghost will recover."

"Great news," the ghost agreed with the slightest trace of enthusiasm. "Ghostly guide—my afterlife's—calling."

Lenny looked around the still quiet comedy club. "We're still safe here?"

"They haven't found us yet," the swami replied.

"Wait!" The Baron stepped forward, dramatically unfurling his cape. "I sense a warning."

He pointed to the wall behind the stage, where an army of cockroaches swirled across the red velvet wallpaper. Dark words formed as the roaches abruptly paused:

you have a moment
but your magic protection
is not forever

"My lovely roaches," the Baron beamed. "They are so useful to have around."

"We must hurry to the next stage of our discovery spell," Phil said. Everyone but Karnowski turned to look at Lenny.

"Where are we?" Phil continued. "Let me review. Swamis are good at summaries. It is a part of our skill set." He pointed to Lenny. "We know the first day cover is of central importance to your gift. Only by reclaiming that cover can we truly understand, and hopefully control, the power that resides within you."

"Sheila stole the first day cover from Lenny, and gave it to her father." Phil waved at the room around him. "Foo is hiding it somewhere. I'm guessing somewhere near.

"We must locate that stamp and turn it to our advantage. This is the secret of Lenny's gift. And we must do it quickly, without delay."

Out of the corner of his eye, Lenny caught a sudden flash of blue from the other side of the room.

"Whoo! What a trip!" Bob the horse popped back into their midst with a whinny of triumph. "Getting out of that dream thing took premier pooka power!"

Lenny shook his head. "That reminds me, wasn't this my dream?

How did Bob end up in the middle of it?"

Phil dipped his head in apology. "There are parts of this process that swamis do not understand."

"Nothing is impossible for pookas!" Bob exclaimed.

"Especially when those parts of the process involve pookas," Phil agreed. "But we have no time for that now. We need to place you back into the trance so that we can find the first day cover."

The swami raised his voice slightly. "My good Karnowski. If I might have your attention."

The ghost finder turned away from his nameless charge. "Karnowski believes he is on mend. Ghosts do not die. They simply fade away."

"We need your help," Phil said. "It is time to summon the ghost of Lenny present. Have you seen any more ghosts that might be of use to us?"

Karnowski scowled. "Wards still too strong. I have no ghosts. But who knows ways of spirit world better than ghost finder? Karnowski will be Lenny's guide."

The swami paused, then nodded. "Unconventional, but I think it will work."

"Hey guys!" Bob the horse called. "We've got something better than ghosts! Ready, willing, and able, over here!"

"I'm afraid that the very nature of pookas . . ." Phil left the rest of the thought unsaid. "Karnowski, you must use your spiritual knowledge to guide Lenny toward his goal."

The swami reached into his Nehru jacket, and once again held the pendant in his hand. "Look at the gem, Lenny."

The jewel swung back and forth before him. The zirconia sparkled, almost as if the gem had an energy of its own.

Lenny already felt his eyes closing.

"You remember your safeguards in the dream state—those things that we discussed before."

"Finger snap," Lenny replied. "Safe word."

"Excellent. Look at the gem and listen to my words."

"Oogleybook," Phil intoned in a low but powerful voice. "Nanglytoot, hocus pocus. Wampo, stampo, oolyompo. You are in my power."

Oolyompo? Lenny thought. What had happened to "Goolyflaspmun?" But the world around him started drifting away.

Phil spoke in a monotone. "Listen to your spirit guide. You seek the first day cover."

"Spirit," Karnowski repeated. "Cover."
"You will find the first day cover," Phil continued.
"Find first day," the ghost finder agreed.
"You will find your power."
"Power," Karnowski echoed.
"Power," Lenny agreed.
The world went dark.

Twenty-One

Lenny opened his eyes. He stood in the center of the comedy club. Everything was totally still, until a voice filled his brain.

"Karnowski is ghost finder of Lenny present!" the voice announced. "Karnowski will help you find true meaning of today, and path forward to tomorrow. Karnowski here to guide way!"

Karnowski's voice was in his ear, but the ghost finder was nowhere to be seen. The rest of the Terrifitemps team had vanished as well. Lenny was alone on the stage. The shelves were still empty, the chairs still piled on tables.

The door to the outside hall was open.

Lenny was back in the trance.

"Think about what is most important to your gift," Karnowski droned on. "Think about your first day cover. Think, and it will call to you."

In the dreamlike quiet around him, Lenny heard the faintest of hums. Was it the letter, or something more? Lenny had to find out.

He started walking, out of the club and down the hall, retracing the path they had taken before. The hum was louder now, more distinct.

Somebody with a white jacket—a technician, perhaps—walked toward him. The other man seemed to look through Lenny, as though Lenny wasn't there. Perhaps he wasn't. Perhaps that was the nature of the trance. In a way, Lenny walked through the real world without being "real" himself.

The hum droned louder still. It was a sonic beacon, leading him to the secret of his gift. Lenny turned the corner and stopped. The stainless steel door before him vibrated with the intensity of the sound.

"Karnowski says open door. Cover lies within."

Lenny did as he was told.

The door opened to a large, chilled room crowded with computers and flat-screen monitors. This had to be the inner sanctum of Foo's secret headquarters. Foo, his daughter and their burly bodyguard sat in three of four ergonomic desk chairs aligned with a long console topped by a dozen screens. Lenny guessed the fourth chair had once been reserved for Swami Phil. Half a dozen technicians busied themselves in other corners of the large room. A couple of them wore the same white lab coat as the man Lenny had passed in the hall. The other four wore the usual robes, royal blue in this case, with a bright yellow "F" embroidered on the right shoulders. A row of hooks holding matching hoods hung on the far wall.

Foo was regarding his daughter critically. Sheila was wearing a form-fitting, dark-gray pantsuit with a scoop neck just low enough to show the slightest hint of cleavage. Lenny had to admit, she looked pretty fabulous.

"Do you really need all these designer fashions?" Foo complained.

"Daddy!" Sheila shot back angrily. "Sometimes I wish Mother had not moved to Miami. Your daughter has to look good if you intend to be a first-class world conqueror. Be glad I don't have a thing about shoes."

Foo sighed. "Do you realize how expensive it is to constantly generate my world-conquering contingency charts? Not to mention the . . ." He paused.

"Is it time, Boss?" Bruno wheeled a man bound to an office chair out from a side door. The man, who was also gagged, wore a soiled white jumpsuit with the letter "S" on the chest. He was Lenny's mystery man; the stranger who had guided Lenny through the tunnels and shown him the way!

"Ignore these individuals!" Karnowski urged. "Look for letter."

The evil genius pointed at his prisoner. "Yes, we will teach people who sneak around our headquarters just what it means to cross Foo! Won't we, Mr. S?"

Whatever their captive replied, it was muffled by the gag.

"And we will discover the secrets of Terrifitemps as well, won't we"—Foo paused for dramatic effect—"Mr. Siggenbottom!"

The captive's muffled cry was much louder and more dramatic this time around.

"Sheila?" Foo asked gently. "If you would reach down beneath that chair and fetch my tool box? It is time to begin work on our prisoner."

But before Sheila could lean over to fetch the box, Foo raised a hand.

"Wait. Something else is here."

Bruno stepped from behind his prisoner, turning his head to stare at every corner of the room. "Something? What do you mean—something?"

Foo turned toward Lenny as he sniffed at the air. "With the swami no longer with us, we have to rely on those supernatural detection skills he taught us."

"But Daddy!" Sheila looked around the room as well. "Something could be anything!"

Lenny frowned. Did Foo somehow know he was here? In the middle of Lenny's own trance? How could these figments of his imagination be reacting to his presence in his dream? And why? He was looking for his special gift. Maybe his special gift was looking for trouble.

Lenny didn't have time for these existential dilemmas. Not when he knew how to make trouble go away.

Lenny snapped his fingers.

"Find letter," Karnowski urged in a hoarse whisper.

"What are you wearing today?" Foo frowned at his daughter. "Your tastes are far too expensive."

"Oh, Daddy!" Sheila rolled her eyes. Her even-more-skin-tight pantsuit was now a hot pink, with maybe a bit more cleavage than her last outfit.

Lenny looked around the room. The captive was gone—was it really Mr. Siggenbottom? And really, who was Mr. Siggenbottom? Husband? Brother? Father? Somebody who only coincidentally had the same last name? It was too much to think about. Lenny needed that letter.

Foo pointed at the third digital monitor from the left, which pictured a forklift grabbing a large crate on a loading dock. He leaned forward to read the logo on the side of the box. "And what is that? A new shipment of shoes?"

"Daddy! Just think of the glossy magazine's special dictators edition!" She pointed one high-heeled boot in her father's direction. "The attention and respect you get from the fashion spreads will be worth every penny."

"It will have to come out of the contingency kickback reserve, but I suppose for my . . . wait a moment. I do not think we are alone."

"Someone else is here?" Bruno demanded. "Where?"

Were they going to discover him all over again?

Lenny had been trying to ignore the chatter and concentrate on the hum. It was emanating from a spot directly behind Foo, in a place high on the console that featured nothing but a blank metal plate. That meant the first day cover was only a few feet away! If he could somehow get inside that console, find the way to open Foo's secret compartment before they discovered any more about Lenny's presence—well, he did have a way, didn't he?

Lenny snapped his fingers.

"The letter?" Karnowski asked.

What? Oh, the letter. Lenny tore his eyes away from Sheila's new outfit, half a dozen strips of neon black and green cloth crisscrossing her frame, showing so much skin the outfit looked more like a bikini than a pantsuit. She towered over her father—her heels had doubled in height.

"Photo shoot?" her father said in a strained voice.

"All Male Dictators Quarterly," Sheila agreed. "But you were saying?"

"How could I forget?" Foo agreed. "We have an intruder in our midst!"

"We can't have that," Sheila said as she bent over to check a dial on the console before her. Lenny found his gaze wandering that way. She turned to her father. "Why don't you check your swami supplies?"

Foo clapped his hands. "Brilliant idea! Sheila, we'll make you an evil genius yet!"

He turned and flipped three seemingly random switches among the hundreds before him. The metal plate on the console slid away, revealing a large hidden recess within.

Lenny imagined he took a step back in surprise. The hum had become so loud it sounded like a rock song from the eighties. Lenny saw two things in the hidden space, a box labeled SWAMI INC., and the first day cover, sealed inside a small glass jar with a rubber cap.

"Get the kit," Foo said, "and see what we can find."

"You have found letter!" Karnowski cheered.

Indeed he had. Now Lenny needed to grab it and run.

Sheila pulled a small silver sphere from the box. "Perhaps the spirit sphere?"

Foo nodded his agreement. "Whoever lurks among us will be trapped in a matter of seconds."

Trapped? Lenny hoped not. Anyway, he didn't plan to stay around long enough for them to trap anything. He stepped around Sheila, his fingers brushing up against her scanty costume. They passed right through, as if Sheila wasn't there. He stood directly in front of the hidden compartment.

"Karnowski says get out of there now!"

"One second." He reached for the letter.

Wait a moment. It wasn't Sheila who wasn't really here, was it? How could Lenny grab the letter if his ghostly hands couldn't touch anything?

The sphere spun in Sheila's hand. "According to the swami, this thing can trap ghosts, astral projections, all sorts of things."

It hummed at an entirely different frequency from the letter, a higher, grating noise. The sound was piercing. Lenny was having trouble concentrating.

"We've got you now!" Foo cackled.

"Is that Lenny?" Sheila asked with a frown.

"It's hard to make out details," Foo agreed.

"Even at the best of times, Lenny was a little indistinct," Sheila agreed.

Lenny looked down at his ghostly self. He was glowing with a faint blue light. He felt like he had been caught in netting, as if something was brushing against his extremities; a web that was growing ever tighter. His legs were pinned together, his arms pressed close by his sides. He could barely move.

He just managed to snap his fingers.

And?

He still couldn't move, not even to turn his head. He couldn't speak. He was truly trapped in his trance state. He could do nothing but watch. Lenny waited. Something always changed when he snapped his fingers.

"We have you where we want you now, Lenny."

Sheila stepped into his field of vision. This time, her scanty costume was made of shiny black leather That seemed to both push together and barely cover the most interesting parts of her body. And she carried a whip.

Foo cleared his throat. "I still don't think those costumes are entirely appropriate for . . ." Words seemed to fail him.

"They're doing a shoot for Dictator's Domination Digest." Sheila cracked the whip inches from Lenny's glowing blue nose. "The publicity will be priceless."

"Lenny!" Karnowski called urgently. "Say word! Say safe word!"

Lenny couldn't open his mouth to say anything.

"What's this?" Foo chuckled. "You've caught something else in your web."

"Karnowski says—" The disembodied voice was garbled now. "Karnow—Kar-onoma—no—ommmmmmmm."

The disembodied voice faded to silence.

"What is this thing?" Foo continued, looking at something outside Lenny's line of sight. Had Karnowski's voice taken physical form? "It doesn't have much shape at all. Can we destroy it along with Lenny?"

"I don't see why not." Sheila rooted around in the swami box. "The vaporizer is in here somewhere." She glanced back at Lenny. "He can't move at all?" She flicked her whip. "Maybe, before we vaporize him, I can spend a few minutes working on my technique."

Foo began to laugh. "We were needlessly worried about this attack. We easily defeated our foes at Terrifitemps! Anything they throw against us, we will overcome. Nothing can stop us now!"

"What am I, chopped liver?" a chipper voice replied.

"I've seen that horse somewhere before!" Foo exclaimed.

"A pooka in need is a horse indeed!" Bob agreed.

Sheila lifted up the sphere before her. "I don't see why this device can't capture pookas as well."

The sphere's whine rose higher in pitch.

"I know that one!" Bob agreed. He began to sing: "I'm pickin' up good vibrations!"

"I don't think this works on pookas," Foo said, his voice a resigned monotone. "Didn't the swami say that nothing worked on pookas?"

Sheila shook her head. "He just said pookas were difficult. Very difficult. Maybe there's something in here." She reached back into the box and pulled out a trade paperback. Lenny read the title: 1,000 Magical Cures Using Common Household Remedies.

Sheila paged quickly through the book.

"Let me just check the index. It would be under 'P.' Pasta, pistons, poltergeists—Here it is! Page 238!" She flipped to the middle of the book and read: "Eliminate unsightly pookas forever!"

"But pookas are your friends!" Bob countered. "Let me give you the top five reasons pookas are a welcome addition to any party—"

"I'll need ammonia," Sheila read from the book. "A couple of chocolate chip cookies. And a large paper bag."

"Oh." Bob paused as Foo's minions assembled everything Sheila rattled off. "If you could just give me a second? Even pookas can benefit from a bit of quiet. Well, not very often, but still—"

"A losing lottery ticket," she continued. "Mayonnaise."

"Mayonnaise and pookas?" Bob actually sounded concerned. "Not the most winning combination. I feel there is something I need to say."

"Ball bearings," Sheila said, "and duct tape."

"Wait a moment!" Bob replied. "It's right on the tip of my tongue. Unomono? Onanoonoo?"

"Put them together!" Sheila ordered her minions as they rushed in from the four corners of the room. "Quickly!" She opened the book to reveal a diagram.

"Why can't I remember—it's like the mambo!" Bob's voice cheered instantly. "Da-da-da-da-da-da!" He whinnied. "That's it!

"Onomatopoeia!" he cried in triumph.

The world went dark.

Twenty-Two

Lenny opened his eyes. He lay flat on his back in the comedy club.

"Are you all right?" It was Lenore's voice. She leaned over him in concern.

"We found the letter," he replied, glad that he could talk again. "But it was far more dangerous than we imagined."

That wasn't what he really meant. The first day cover wasn't dangerous by itself; it was everything that happened around the letter. Lenny did his best to explain, giving a quick summary to Lenore, Swami Phil, and the Baron. Like how his finger snapping seemed mostly to get Sheila to change clothes (Lenore seemed to frown a bit during his descriptions of the wardrobe), until one final snap led to the revelation of the first day cover. Which was in turn followed by his frustration with not being able to actually grab it and run.

Swami Phil nodded his head in admiration.

"You have had the most remarkable trance states that I have ever witnessed. Still, there are aspects of this process that I find worrisome. In both the past and present hypnotic events, problems escalated around you until even the complications had complications."

A loud groan erupted to Lenny's left. He sat up, and saw the ghost finder collapsed at the side of the stage.

"Karnowski cannot breathe," the ghost finder rasped. "Karnowski needs rest."

"We have our momentary casualties," Phil acknowledged. "I believe both our ghost and our ghost finder will recover. But this situation leads to further concerns.

"Even though Lenny survives relatively unscathed, each of these trance events has veered ever closer toward chaos. Despite my earlier plans, I am afraid it would be too dangerous to attempt the final third of my original spell."

"Then no ghost of Lenny yet to come?" Lenore asked.

Phil nodded. "The last spell might be beneficial, but it will have to wait. Besides, we have located the first day cover. And we have another method of obtaining it."

He grinned at the others. "It's time for a full frontal assault, with a little help, swami style. Allow me to explain." He waved to the stage. "First, the letter and Lenny are intertwined. Whatever we do, Lenny has to be a part of this."

He turned to look at Lenny. "Are you up for this?"

Lenny nodded. Aside from a bit if dizziness when he first woke up, he felt fine.

"Then we will simply grab the letter and get out of Foo's secret hideout. The last third of your trance can wait until we're in a safer place."

"Wait!" the Baron interrupted. "My pets have a message!"

Lenny and the others turned to see the roaches milling about on the nearest wall. They spelled new words, black letters swirling against the red.

*foo has regained
control of his security
better get moving!*

Phil nodded. "No time for subtlety, then. We'll have to do the old swami smash and grab."

"But what about Foo's minions?" Lenore asked. "Won't they try to stop us?"

"Not if they can't see us." The swami studied his hands. "I think I can manage a contact invisibility spell with a minimum of fuss."

Lenny decided someone had to ask the question. "A contact invisibility spell?'

"A spell where the primaries stay invisible, as long as they stay in physical contact," the swami explained. "I will be at the center of the spell. We'll go in with one of you to either side of me."

"Just two?" Lenore looked to the others in the room. "Lenny has to come. Who gets left behind?"

"Karnowski cannot stand!" the ghost hunter groaned from his fetal position on the floor.

"I'm on the mend! I can maintain my physical form for upwards of two—" The nameless ghost flickered out and then back into existence.

"Well, maybe a minute and a half."

"Both of them are better left behind." The Baron dismissed Lenore's concerns with a flick of his cape. "And as for me, I need no invisibility spells. I am a vampire. I will arrive as a chilling evening mist."

Phil nodded his approval. "Hopefully that will add to the confusion."

He waved to the others. "Lenore! Lenny! To my sides. We must clasp hands. Then we must move swiftly." Lenny took Phil's right hand while Lenore clasped his left. Phil said a few more words that made no particular sense. Lenny guessed it was the usual magic mumbo jumbo.

"I can see none of you!" the Baron called.

"We can see each other, but no one else can see us. Unless we are separated." He let go of Lenny and Lenore's hands.

"And now I can see both!" the Baron agreed.

"Good," the swami agreed. "We all know the parameters of the spell. Grab my hand again, and let's get that first day cover."

Phil led the way, pulling the two others through the door. They rushed once more down the hallway Lenny had traveled in his trance. Another young man in a lab coat passed them without glancing their way. They turned the final corner that led to Foo.

"We're in luck," Phil whispered. "The door is open." He led the two others, more slowly than before, into Foo's inner chamber. More than a dozen men and women, some in lab coats, some in robes, were busily typing at workstations. A few were clustered at the far side of the room, studying flowcharts displayed on a large wall screen.

They crept silently through the crowd. So far, no one seemed to notice them at all.

They crept closer to Foo and his daughter. Beyond the two of them, Lenny knew, was the secret compartment that held the first day cover.

Sheila glared at her father. "Not another word about my outfit!" This time, her stylish pantsuit held three well-spaced holes, each strategically revealing a patch of skin beneath. "You wouldn't talk to me that way if Mother were still here."

"I told you I never want to talk about your mother," Foo snapped. "We don't have time for this argument. The security cameras are functioning again, and we've located our enemy."

"Where?" Sheila asked.

"They're hiding in the comedy club."

"We have a comedy club?"

"It was never finished," Foo admitted. "I just don't find—well, that's not important. Bruno, I need you to take a detail of security personnel down the hall."

The burly head of security stepped forward to meet with Foo. But before either of them could say anything, they were interrupted by a song.

"You're my lover! You're my lover!"

Lenny recognized the ringtone.

"Someone is calling you here?" Foo demanded. "Now?"

Sheila glanced at her phone. "It's more of an alarm, really. The swami installed an intruder app a couple weeks back. Something just set it off."

"We have an intruder?" Bruno asked.

"You're my lover! You're my lover!" the phone agreed.

Sheila nodded. "We can't see anybody, but we are not alone."

"They can sense us even though we're invisible?" Lenore whispered.

"I'm too thorough for my own good," the swami whispered back.

"Bruno!" Foo shouted. "Call the entire security team in here. This room must be searched first." He turned to look around the busy area. "Who could come in here without being seen? It has to be the swami."

"Or Lenny," Sheila added, frowning at the room in turn. "When something strange happens, it's always Lenny."

"We know you're here," Foo said in a loud voice. "Why not show yourself?"

"Lenny!" Phil whispered, in a tone just above the low hum of the surrounding computers. "Lead us toward the letter. We have to get out of here."

"Is it you, swami?" Foo continued. "You left us so suddenly, we haven't had a chance to cancel your benefits package."

"Lenny?" Sheila countered. "Is it you? Maybe I don't want to kill you right away. Maybe we really need to talk." She hugged her arms close to her chest. "Is it getting a little clammy in here?"

"You wouldn't be cold if you wore clothes that covered more of your body!" her father chided.

Lenny saw the mist congeal around Sheila's ankles. She shuddered. The Baron had arrived.

Lenore, Lenny, and Phil inched closer to the console directly behind Foo and Sheila.

"You can come back to us, Swami!" Foo continued. "Your old job is waiting for you. No hard feelings. Once we've conquered the world, your piece of the profit sharing should be phenomenal."

"It is tempting." The swami hesitated. "But no," he continued, still in a whisper. "I am on the frontiers of swami science." He pointed to the console. "How do we get this thing open?"

"Simple. Foo threw three switches." Lenny looked at the hundreds of switches on the console before him. Which were the right three?

"Lenny? Talk to me!" Sheila insisted. "This is your last last chance. I really mean it this time."

"Swami, you left too soon," Foo insisted. "Not only will we defeat our enemies, but we will achieve total synergistic integration throughout our entire organization!"

"Don't worry," Phil whispered in Lenny's ear. "Even I don't know what that means."

"Hey guys," Lenore cut in with a whisper of her own. "Can't we get the first day cover and get out of here?"

"Lenny just has to throw the correct switches," Phil replied.

Lenny wondered if he could trust in his gift to pick out the right combination. But what would happen if he got the sequence wrong?

"I've got the security detail!" Bruno called from the hallway door.

"Excellent!' Foo clapped his hands sharply. "Minions! Leave your stations. Line up in a row along the far wall. Security, you will fan out from the door and cover every inch of empty space between you and the minions. When you encounter something you can feel but cannot see—and I believe there are more then one of those invisible beings in the room—show it no mercy!"

Lenny swore silently. It was high time his gift did something.

Somebody screamed.

"Hey, Lenny! How's tricks?"

Lenny turned from the console. The pooka had materialized midair, in the very center of the room.

So Bob had arrived. But from where? Lenny thought about the last time he had seen the pooka, when Bob had gotten himself right into the middle of his second trance. Lenny's trance, he thought, until Bob showed up.

Bob kicked up his heels with an energetic whinny. "Wow! These swami spells can turn a pooka inside out. But I'm back!"

"It's a talking blue horse," Sheila remarked. "Now I'm sure Lenny is in the room."

"Yeah!" Bob agreed enthusiastically. "Lenny? I know you're here somewhere, too. Nobody can hide from a pooka!"

"Quick!" Foo shouted. "We don't have time for security. Grab the swami scope from the secret compartment. We'll trap them all!"

Foo leaned forward to flip the correct switches. The secret compartment opened once again. Lenny inched forward, careful not to brush against Sheila. The hidden compartment, and the first day cover, were almost within reach. If he could just lean forward a little . . .

Lenny yelped. Bob's blue snout was inches from his nose.

"There you are!" the pooka cheered. "A little tough to see, maybe. But not for your friend Bob!"

Lenny stumbled forward, losing his grip on Phil's hand. He fell awkwardly against the console.

"Lenny!" Sheila called by his side. "See, Daddy? I knew he was here."

Lenny pushed himself away from the console. He had to ignore Sheila, ignore Bob, ignore everything except for the first day cover.

"And he's not alone!" Sheila crowed.

Lenore popped into sight on the other side of Sheila, only a few feet away. The invisible swami must still be somewhere in between.

"Dad!" Sheila pointed triumphantly at the Terrifitemps psychic. "Here's that melodramatic witch that Lenny's been hanging out with."

"Melodramatic?" Lenore glanced down at her all-black costume before glaring back at Sheila. "At least I don't dress like a slut in some grade-Z spy movie!"

The two women grabbed at each other.

"Wait!" a commanding voice came from Sheila's side. "This has gone far enough!" The mist solidified to form the Baron.

Foo gasped. "You! I thought I'd never see you again."

The Baron shrugged. "I've got a new job. Even vampires have to eat."

Sheila paused in her girl fight to stare at the vampire. "You two know each other?"

Foo nodded, perhaps a bit reluctantly. "We made a deal, some time ago."

The Baron smiled slightly, showing the tips of his fangs. "Last time our paths crossed, I was not so gainfully employed. You had a certain—problem—you had to deal with." He glanced at Sheila. "And what a pretty daughter! Lucky for you, my dear, that you favor your mother."

Sheila glared back at her father. "How would a vampire know anything about my mother?"

"I only did what I was paid to do." The Baron sighed wistfully. "Before this happened, I never thought I could have enough vampire brides. Proves even the undead can be wrong now and then."

"You had this vampire? Mother?" Sheila couldn't finish a sentence. She looked from her father to the Baron and back again. "You mean Mother really isn't in Miami?"

Foo offered his daughter a resigned smile. "Sheila. You, I can deal with. Your mother, not so much."

Sheila had become the center of attention. Nobody in the room was looking at Lenny.

He grabbed the first day cover.

It was still in its protective jar, but just by putting his hand around the glass, Lenny felt a jolt of energy snake up his arm and shoulder.

"Wait!" His sudden movement had attracted Foo's attention. The evil genius pointed straight at Lenny. "Put that down now!"

"Oh boy!" Bob the horse called. "Now thing's are going to get really interesting!"

Somewhere, in the distance, Lenny could hear a herd of buffalo, singing.

Twenty-Three

Time seemed to slow around Lenny. The world surrounding him still moved. Heads turned toward him, hands reached in his direction, but they did so with the exquisite slowness of a late sixties action film.

Lenny held something in his hands—something much more immediate. The first day cover called to him, entreating him to open the jar and hold the paper in his hands.

Lenny realized he hadn't actually touched the valuable artifact, his skin brushing against paper, since that day in his childhood when he had first slid the letter into its plastic sheath. He knew now that was the moment his talent first manifested, if only in small ways at the beginning. His gift had blossomed over the years. Where it had at first brought small events—some perhaps, not even noticed—to his door, the occasions had become larger and stranger and decidedly more dramatic over time. Upon reflection, Lenny realized that having a meteor destroy your workplace was about as dramatic as you could get.

Lenny's mind danced from one unexplained event to another, from that minor earthquake in the middle of the night of his senior prom to the day the post office delivered 317 copies of Reader's Digest. And then there were those mermaids and talking animals (well before Bob the horse) and various other fantastic creatures. Not to mention the singing buffalo.

And, now that Lenny held the letter in his hand, the buffalo were back.

His strange talent had grown over the years. What would happen if he physically held the letter in his hands right now?

He saw Foo slowly fumble with one of the swami's special devices, something sort of like (but not quite) whatever it was that had trapped him in his trance—had that only happened a few moments before? Things were occurring much faster than they ever had.

Lenny frowned in concentration. He wanted to avoid anything that Foo might do to him, ever again. And what else? With a sudden clarity,

Lenny's goals popped one after another into his mind.

First, he needed to prevent Foo from prevailing.

Second, he needed to rescue his Terrifitemps team.

Third, he needed to find a way to restore Ms. Siggenbottom and Withers to their former, sane selves. And maybe rescue Mr. Siggenbottom as well. (And he couldn't forget about the werevole.)

Fourth (although maybe this should rank higher), he needed a way to get Sheila out of his life once and for all. Forever. Permanently.

And maybe, just maybe, he needed a way forward, with his gift, with his job, and maybe even with Lenore, if she would have him.

Lenny took a deep breath. He knew of only one way to make these things possible.

He unscrewed the lid of the jar.

Lenny looked up as the lid pulled free. Foo was screaming in slow motion. Sheila was yelling directly at him, just as slowly, telling him to stop, he didn't know what he was—Well, he didn't have time to listen to the whole slow sentence. The time to act was now.

He reached in to pull the letter from the jar. His finger touched the edge of the envelope. The electric charge that had run up his arm before jolted through his entire body.

Lenny blinked.

It was so close. The whole world, and other, larger things beyond the world. Images flooded his mind; things he had forgotten, small, magical incidents on the edge of sleep; the morning an extra sun had risen in the west, to fade from view a few seconds later; the rocket ship that would visit him in his ten-year-old-child dreams, until that morning he woke up and saw a replica of the ship sitting on the night table beside his bed. He still had that tiny ship on a bookshelf in his apartment. How could he have forgotten where it had come from?

Lenny saw further still, wondering at oceans made of light, great fields of grain where every stalk sang in perfect harmony, and glimpsing large, lumbering things that faded in and out of the night.

He didn't remember those. Was he seeing things that hadn't happened yet?

Lenny heard a loud crack, like some giant plastic toy being broken in half.

Time sped up to normal.

"Security!" Lenny heard Foo shout. "Get that letter away from him!"

Bruno and the others weren't paying any attention to their boss. They were still busy slowly walking across the room, waving their arms around in search of additional invisible visitors. Besides, Foo was having trouble being heard over the noise.

The buffalo were at the door. And their singing was, if anything, even more boisterous than before.

"I want a girl, just like the girl, that married dear old dad."

"Lenny!" Sheila shouted, opening her arms in entreaty. "You don't know how to handle that letter!"

The buffalo sang on:

"She was a pearl and the only girl that Daddy ever had!"

"And you do?" Lenore demanded of Sheila. "I bet Lenny can handle"—she paused for a second to pick just the right words—"just about anything better than you!"

"A good old-fashioned girl with heart so true!" the buffalo boisterously bounced along.

"Oh yeah?" Sheila yelled.

"One who loves nobody else but you!" the herd thundered.

"Yeah!" Lenore shouted back.

The women started pushing each other again.

"I want a girl..."

"Sheila!" Foo commanded. "Stop!"

Foo yelled as his daughter pushed him out of the way.

"I've got this, Boss!" Bruno yelled back.

"Just like the girl..."

Bruno staggered as Lenore hit the top of his head with a handy iPad.

"...that married dear—old—daddddddd!"

Everyone froze. The end of the buffalo's song plunged the room into an instant of total silence.

In the sudden stillness, Lenny could see the large room was changing. He spotted new faces in the crowd. Faces that came from his gift. New sounds erupted from different quarters of Foo's lair.

The left side of the room was totally enthralled by a trio of singing mermaids.

Another group—mostly security guards—were being bashed on the head by a very merry troll.

Huh. Lenny had completely forgotten about the troll.

"Hey, Lenny!" A short man in a dirty jumpsuit with the letter "S" sewn on the chest stood before him. "Thanks for having that horse show me how to get out of that trap!"

"Pooka at your service!" Bob beamed.

A woman in a lab coat rushed in from the corridor. "We better stay in here! There's a meteor shower in the hall!"

Meteors in the hallway? Did the buffalo have to scatter?

Lenny saw that the Baron had taken an attractive young lab assistant in his arms and was baring his fangs. From the lab assistant's dreamy smile, she did not appear to be particularly upset.

Bruno, still holding his head, staggered toward the vampire. "And what do you call this?" the security chief demanded.

"Lunch," the Baron admitted.

Lenny whistled softly. How could this get any more chaotic?

The swami abruptly popped into view.

"Lenny!" Swami Phil screamed. "You have to stop this now."

"What?" Lenny replied. He could only stop this if he knew how it got started in the first place.

The troll loomed above Swami Phil, his large and gnarly club held high in the air.

"Bodder Lenny?" the troll asked.

Lenny remembered now. When the troll had first appeared all those years ago, right in the middle of an encounter with some schoolyard bullies, he and Lenny had become fast friends.

Lenny shook his head. "No bother Lenny."

"Troll Lenny's friend!" The huge creature nodded back and smiled a mostly toothless grin.

Maybe, in a way, all the visitors brought by his gift were Lenny's friends.

"All your manifestations are coming together!" Phil shouted at the once-more rising sea of noise. "It's too much power! Your gift could tear apart the very fabric of reality!"

Really? Lenny's first thought was that sounded kind of cool. And how would his friends go about destroying the world, anyway? But his second thought was that he had no way to sew it back together again.

Wasn't the swami overreacting to all of this? Maybe the two of them could talk this out, come up with some reasonable solution.

But, instead of saying that, Lenny found strange words bubbling out of his mouth.

"Oogleybook," Lenny spoke as if something outside himself was forcing his lips to move.

"No! Not that!" Phil clutched at his collar as the large cubic zirconia floated up on the end of its chain, freeing itself from within the Nehru jacket.

"Nanglytoot," Lenny's voice continued, "Osh kosh by gosh. Urpim, burpim, snagglelurpim!"

"The third spell is starting on its own!" Phil grabbed at the medallion as it swung back and forth in front of Lenny. The swami made strangling noises as the chain whipped around his neck. "We may still—be able to—stop it. Spell can't—complete without—a spirit guide." He swiped at the chain. "Both ghost and Karnowski—are still not here. Maybe it—will—just—fizzle out."

Bob the horse leaned over Phil's shoulder. "Spirit guide? Is it my turn at last?"

Phil gasped for air. The chain was so tangled around the swami's neck that speaking was beyond him.

What could Lenny do? Except to watch the jewel sparkle, back and forth, back and forth. He was getting drowsy.

"I am the ghost of Lennies yet to come!" Bob giggled. "I've always wanted to do this!"

The swami gagged and struggled. Bob danced. The zirconia sparkled and spun.

Was something terrible going to happen? Or was this what was always meant to be? Either way, Lenny couldn't keep his eyes open.

The world was lost in swirling mist.

Twenty-Four

He was still in Foo's control room. But the lab around him was totally still.

"This is the legacy of Lenny's future!" Bob called out of the gloom. "This is the direction your life will take if you remain on your present course. Heed you well, lest you come to this sad—hey, who writes this stuff, anyway?"

So Bob wasn't going to be able to follow the script. Lenny wasn't sure if that should be reassuring or not.

Something groaned from amid the swirling vapors.

"What's with all this fog?" he could hear Foo shouting. "This air-filtration system cost me big bucks!"

Foo yelped as a large, half-seen shape moved in front of him.

Lenny almost yelped in turn as two very large somethings stepped out of the gloom.

No, he was wrong. It was one extremely large something. With two heads. One of the heads was definitely male, with a receding hairline and a beard. The other head appeared to be female, with flowing blonde hair and ruby lips.

"How about that dramatic entrance, huh?" the male head rumbled. "That never fails to get their attention!"

The female head frowned at that. "You always have to talk first, don't you?"

"Thank you, Lenny!" The first head apparently chose to ignore the second's remarks. "Your actions will lead us ever closer to triumph."

"Triumph?' the female head sneered. "I don't know why Mother ever said you were good with words. Lenny, your actions shall finally lead us to our goal, the total subjugation of the human race!"

"This is a pretty crappy future!" Foo yelled from somewhere deep in the mists. "What happens to all my well-laid plans?"

"What happens is silence!" the male head rumbled.

Foo yelped and spoke no more.

"Know this, Lenny," the male head continued. "We found you were special. And we guided your every discovery, and showed you the way to power. We are your reason for being."

"We haven't introduced ourselves," the female head interjected.

"Of course," the male head interrupted in turn. "Know this. We are among the most ancient of beings. While great pantheons of immortals fought against the unspeakable terrors that now sleep in places with unpronounceable names, we waited. While ancient civilizations rose and fell, grew famous throughout the known world and then passed from memory, we waited. We are the other immortals, those who will emerge triumphant when all others are pummeled to dust. We are the Overlooked, and we wait no more."

"The Overlooked?" Swami Phil enthused from somewhere nearby. "Wow! Who knew your talent would bring this? I wonder how we can use—"

The swami yelped, and spoke no more.

"We will let you speak, or not," the male head intoned.

"We will let you live, or not," the female head added.

Whatever these things were, they were slowly, one by one, silencing those around Lenny. They said they showed Lenny the way to power, but did they control that power? Or was Lenny in control—a control he was only now beginning to realize?

Lenny knew of one way to find out. He snapped his fingers.

He heard the buffalo singing, somewhere in the fog:

"Oh Susanna, now don't you cry for me! 'Cause I come from Alabama with a banjo on my knee!"

"Already," the male head acknowledged. "Lenny's power reasserts itself around us. And we will control that power, and Lenny Hodge, absolutely."

"But we still haven't introduced ourselves—really," the female head continued. "We are called by the most ancient of names, Hector and Lucille."

"Are introductions all that important?" complained the male head; Lenny guessed that was Hector.

"I just thought it would be nice for Lenny to know who he was working for," Lucille retorted. "Especially since we will be using his power to bring the cosmos to its knees."

"Does the cosmos actually have knees?" the other head asked.

"It's always been this way!" Lucille cried, flinging her long hair away from her face. "You can talk on a grand scale, but whenever I start, it's nitpick, nitpick, nitpick!"

"I come from Alabama with a banjo on my knee," the buffalo chorused: *"I'm going to Louisiana my true love for to see!"*

"Lenny!" Lenore called. "You don't have to let them do this. They are in your trance. You are in control. Use your safe—"

Another yelp. Another silence.

"What are all these interruptions?" Hector rumbled. "We are the Overlooked, but we will be talked over no more."

"Not by common humans!" the Baron cried. "But newly fed vampires are—"

The Baron yelped as well.

Lenny didn't want to see all his compatriots fall one by one. But what could he do, except snap his fingers?

He did so again. The next time the buffalo sang a line, the mermaids sang in harmony.

"It rained all night the day I left, the weather it was dry!"

"Should we silence the music as well?" Lucille asked.

"I think not. It has been so long since we have been able to gloat, it's nice to be able to do so with musical accompaniment. And the music comes from Lenny's power, soon to be ours as well."

"The sun so hot I froze to death," the buffalo and mermaids all sang in magnificent harmony. *"Susanna don't you cry!"*

Lucille actually chuckled at that. "Sometimes we work so closely together, we forget what we can do. This is proceeding even better than I thought."

"Isn't it? First, we thought we'd introduce ourselves and acquaint Lenny with the inevitability of his fate. That's what a future trance like this is for. But consider the possibilities—"

"Here he goes again," Lucille complained. "Do you know how hard it is to live with somebody whose specialty is long-winded explanation? Maybe if I could take a vacation, I could see things in perspective." She looked disdainfully over at her other head. "But no!"

"Hey, what about the pooka of Lennies yet to come?" Bob the horse spoke up. "Aren't you forgetting something here?"

"Everybody wants to forget about pookas," Lucille agreed.

"Oh yeah?" Bob said. "Well, onoma—"

Bob yelped.

"It takes a little extra effort, but we can silence pookas as well," Hector said. "But as I was saying, think on it—The other deities are trapped in other realms, or have crumbled to dust. Raw power, raw hate, raw fear, all have passed away. But the Overlooked wield the one force that truly controls the universe. Unbridled passive aggression!"

Lucille nodded at last. "Why do we have to tell anybody any more of our plans? Why don't we forget all about this trance business and take over the cosmos now?"

So the secret power behind Lenny's fate would ramble on forever. He had lost all his allies to their mystic might. And, apparently, if he didn't do something soon, his trance state would become the new reality for—well, everybody—and the Overlooked would take complete control.

But Lenny had not tried to speak. He hadn't used the power of his own voice, in his own trance, to end the madness.

"Enough of this!" he said. "Onomat—"

Lenny yelped. He could no longer move his lips. He wasn't even sure if he still had lips to move.

"Et tu, Lenny?" Hector said with great weariness. "Nobody truly knows the hardships of all-powerful entities."

The buffalo and mermaids started in on another chorus. The twin heads bopped along to the beat.

"Oh, Susanna!" Hector sang along. He was back to gloating. "Poor Lenny, I'm afraid you'll have to watch in silence as all your magical creatures swarm around you. You'll be witness to your magic, but still powerless before our might. We will use your power, for we gave it to you, for safekeeping I suppose, until it was time for the Overlooked to wield it once again. Now your gift—our gift, really—will spread from your trance state to take over and reshape what you see as the real world. Until you, too, are consumed by the greatness that is the Overlooked."

So that was Lenny's legacy? He had been a convenient container for tremendous power; power that was about to destroy Lenny and everything he had ever cared about.

Lenny looked from one head to the other and back again. He still couldn't say a thing.

Lenny still had his fingers. What the heck. One final snap.

"Hey dere, Lenny!" The troll ambled out of the fog. Lenny had held some faint hope that he might use this fellow as a weapon against the demigods. But as tall as this product of Lenny's imagination was, the two-headed Hector/Lucille towered over the troll by a good six feet.

"Another of his fantastic creatures?" It was Hector's turn to laugh. "One last entertainment before the world becomes eternally ours! Even if we don't do anything with it!"

The troll looked entreatingly at Lenny.

"Do you know the way to the west woom?" he entreated.

Wow, Lenny thought. Did his talent create fully functional creatures, or what? It was a shame that, now that reality as he knew it was ending, Lenny wouldn't have more time to appreciate his power, his creations, his own real life story. Still, he wouldn't want the troll to suffer in what little time they had left. While Lenny might not be able to talk, he could still wave in the proper direction.

"Thanks, Lenny," the troll replied cheerfully. "Omma gotta peea!"

The two-headed Overlooked screamed as one as Lenny's gift once again saved the day, and the final, future trance faded to black.

Twenty-Five

Lenny wondered afterward if the last part was a dream. How the Overlooked had vanished, leaving Lenny and his teammates surrounded by the legions of Foo. And, at that moment, how Lenny had known.

It was all so simple. He had known what to do, where to go, what it was all about.

Lenny whistled, and a great wind blew his enemies to the ground. He nodded, and the rest of Terrifitemps followed him from the room. He smiled, and was met by a company of singing buffalo, who guided them all from Foo's lair.

So Lenny knew—what? For the life of him, he couldn't remember.

Lenny awoke in the board room of Terrifitemps. He had no idea how he had gotten here, or exactly what had happened in the last few hours. Well, there had been that dream . . .

Images kept floating through his mind; walking through tunnels and parking lots and strangely empty hotels until they had stumbled upon the headquarters of Foo. He could hear arguments he had had with Sheila, and demands he had heard from Foo. He remembered that Sheila was Foo's daughter. That was probably too shocking to forget.

There seemed to be something after that, too, but for now his memory was hazy, half formed, as if whatever had happened next was too large, or maybe too frightening, for his mind to hold. He looked around the room. The rest of his Terrifitemps team sat around him. The remainder of the large space was empty of everything save the large table and a few dozen chairs.

"I seem to have lost ghost somewhere," Karnowski the Ghost Finder remarked dourly.

Lenore looked over all their heads, as though she was searching for something far away. "It feels as if we have all been through a great shock. The swami was helping us, I remember that. Lenny was put into a trance, and then—something dangerous and terrible happened."

Lenore glanced at Lenny, a strange, sad smile on her face. Lenny wondered where that smile came from. Was it part of those things he couldn't remember?

"Lenny was in the middle of it somehow. He almost lost everything." Lenore's smile faltered. "But then he saved us. Somehow."

Lenny guessed everything Lenore said was true, though he couldn't remember any of the details. It had something to do with his particular talents. What were they again—exactly?

Everyone sat in silence for a long moment.

Lenore spoke first. "I do have some good news. Somebody has left me this book." She lifted an oversized paperback from the table. The title was large and easy to read: *1,000 Magical Cures Using Common Household Remedies*.

She put the book back down. Everyone stared into space.

"Karnowski says something must be done!"

The dour fellow lifted the receiver of a black phone with a rotary dial and ordered takeout. "Is best food in neighborhood," Karnowski assured Lenny.

They didn't talk much until the bags of food arrived. Lenny wondered if they were all as exhausted as he was.

The team members dug into the paper and plastic containers. Whatever Lenny had been doing these last few hours, he was famished, too.

The Baron sat quietly by one side. "I am not hungry at all. I seem to have eaten recently." He stood and straightened his cape. "Perhaps I should visit my wives. I feel I have been away far longer than I should have been." He nodded at the others and headed for the elevator that led to his underground lair.

"Karnowski found ghost," the ghost finder mused, "and then lost ghost. But ghosts have way of coming back. Karnowski know that better than anyone."

Lenny tried to put his own thoughts in order. He did remember a fellow in a turban, and a spinning, glittering, fascinating jewel. His talent had done something bad. But then it had made everything right again. Besides that, what did he need to know?

Oh, some animals had been singing, but that was nothing new in his life. He knew he was forgetting something. Something very important.

Lenore put down her plastic fork and asked for the phone. She dialed only three digits. Lenny guessed it was an in-house call. She spoke briefly with whoever was on the other end.

Lenore hung up the phone and looked at Lenny and Karnowski.

"We've had enough time to eat and rest. We still have to rescue two of our fellow Terrifitempers. Since the Baron's already left us, of course, it's up to the three of us, and this book"—she waved the paperback—"to make things right."

Lenore led Lenny and Karnowski down a corridor Lenny had never seen before. They stopped before a formidable steel door. Lenore pressed a button to one side of the entryway and said her name into an intercom. A loud buzzing sounded from the door lock. Lenore pulled the handle toward her and waved both Lenny and Karnowski in ahead of her.

They walked down a short hallway with a couple of nondescript and empty offices to either side. At the end of the hall was a single desk, above which Lenny could see the top of a white-haired head, nothing else. As they grew closer, he realized that the head was attached to a body; a very short body in a very bright printed dress. The hair atop her head was indeed very white, which complemented her wrinkled and frail form. The woman looked old enough to be the grandmother of Lenny's grandmother.

"Lenore," the old woman said without expression as the three of them approached.

"Estelle," Lenore acknowledged in turn. "How are our patients?"

Estelle shook her head. "No real change. Ms. Siggenbottom still babbles on about corn dogs and the like. And Withers is very busy being a vole."

"Are they eating?"

"No problem there. Withers is subsisting mostly on grass, but he did perk up when I found him a dead mouse. And Ms. S. only asks for one thing."

"Corn dogs."

Estelle nodded. "Every couple hours. The kitchen has just sent up number fourteen."

Lenore nodded in turn. "I'm hoping we can speed up recovery for both of them. We need access to the padded cells." She showed Estelle the Magical Cures book.

"Worth a try," the old woman agreed. She turned and pointed to three more steel doors, set side by side in a wall some twenty paces behind her.

"Ms. S. is in number one, Withers in number three. We left the middle one vacant so they wouldn't hear each other quite so much."

Terrifitemnps actually had padded cells on site? How big was this place, anyway? It reminded Lenny of Foo's lair, and how the Terrifitemps team had hidden. In the comedy club? It was all starting to come back to him.

Lenore looked back at her team members. "Let's work on Withers first. We don't know how reliable this book could be. We don't want to make any mistakes. If something were to go wrong . . ."

Lenore left the end of the sentence hanging in the air. But even Lenny understood why they were starting with a nonessential member of the team. Should their first experiment on Withers succeed, it was all to the good. If, on the other hand, there were unforeseen and perhaps even deadly consequences, well, it would be a shame. But then they still could find other, safer avenues to cure the head of their company, Ms. Siggenbottom.

Lenny supposed that, when the time came, he might be expendable as well. As he remembered more and more of his adventures with Foo, he realized that he had been taking a leader's role more and more often. Now that he had returned to Terrifitemps, however, he was back being an underling who knew next to nothing.

Lenore walked past the desk, heading for the three doors. Lenny and Karnowski followed, until all three stood before a door marked "3"—a large, white numeral in the middle of the steel plate. Lenore turned and nodded to Estelle. The door opened with a loud buzz, and the three of them entered the padded cell.

The cell was bright white, illuminated by a string of fluorescent bulbs strung across the high ceiling. The room had no furniture. It was completely empty, save for Withers, who was huddled in the far corner of the room. He lifted his round and furry head, sniffing at the air.

"Squee," he announced. "Squee, squee!"

In the bright light, Lenny realized, the werevole was simply a very large rodent. Sprung upon an unsuspecting public, a werevole might be startling, but he certainly wasn't scary.

"There, there, now Withers," Lenore spoke in a soothing voice. "We're here to help you."

"Squee?" Withers replied in what Lenny thought was a pleading tone.

Lenore glanced at her co-workers. "I don't think Withers will give us any trouble. Let's look in the book."

She opened the *1,000 Magical Cures Using Common Household Remedies*, flipping back to a few pages from the end. "It's got to be in the index somewhere." She turned a couple more pages. "Here we go:

"Spells, reversal of." She flipped forward a few pages. "It goes on for six pages in the index. Let's see if there's anything in here for werevoles."

Werevoles? That sounded a little too specific to Lenny, but then, what did he know?

"Ah!" Sheila announced after a moment's browsing. "Were spells, reversal of full-time transformation."

She felt along the side of her stylish yet gothic-inspired black pantsuit, and pulled out a small pad and pencil from a hidden pocket. She wrote two short lists on two consecutive pages, then ripped the papers from the pad so she could hand them to Karnowski.

"Get Estelle to call down to the kitchen and have these delivered," she said of the first page, then showed him the second. "And you should be able to find these things in one of the desks out there."

She looked at Lenny as the ghost finder left the cell.

"Ask Estelle to show you the broom closet. We'll need a mop and a bucket. Come right back, and we'll get ready. When Karnowski returns, we're going to put it all together. I'm going to recite the spell, but you're going to do the actual mixing of ingredients."

Karnowski ran back into the room, carrying a handful of paper clips, a ragged old phone book (the date on the cover was 1997), and a stapler. "Estelle says the food is on the way up. I'll bring it right back."

Lenore nodded and smiled. Lenny decided he liked working with Lenore.

He guessed the sandwich was tuna on rye, and the wrapped package clearly identified its contents as peanut butter crackers. Whatever was in the pitcher Karnowski carried was steaming. Lenny looked at the last plate and wondered if it specifically had to be lime Jell-O.

Lenore turned to Withers. "Could you please step into the middle of the room?"

The werevole squeed his consent and hopped across the padded floor. Karnowski, his work done, took a step back to watch the proceedings.

Lenny concentrated on following Lenore's instructions exactly, and did his best to keep any other thoughts out of his head. They worked quickly together, until Lenny shoved the mop into the bubbling mixture they had poured into the pail. He pushed the mop vigorously around in the soup, then pulled it out and swiped the wet mop-end once across Withers's forehead.

The transformation was almost instantaneous, dark hair receding to reveal pink skin beneath. A lot of pink skin.

"Oh," Lenore remarked. "Tell Estelle we need a blanket."

But the old woman was already at the door, blanket in hand. Lenore quickly draped it over the shivering Withers, who clutched it tight around him to cover as much of his body as possible.

"Where am I?" He blinked at Lenny. "Oh yes, Mr. Hodge. We just met, didn't we?"

Well, just before the transformation spell, Lenny thought. Who knew how much time had passed since then?

"We'll explain it all later," Lenore didn't explain. "First we need to cure Ms. Siggenbottom." She waved at the paraphernalia scattered across the floor. "Let's take our work into the other cell."

The Terrifitemps team, now including Withers, marched over to the other cell, and waited a moment for Estelle to open the door.

Lenore glanced over at Lenny while they were waiting.

"That was very well done, Lenny. I think you're capable of great things." She smiled at him. "We just have to find some way to get it out of you."

Lenny found himself smiling back. He really hoped the two of them could work on just about everything together.

Ms. Siggenbottom spun toward the door as soon as it opened.

"Get them while they're hot!" she shouted. "Get them while they're hot! Giant economy corn dog!" Unlike Withers and his fur coat, Ms. S. was still dressed in the gray business suit she had been wearing when the spell had overtaken her.

"Yummy, hot corn dog!" She looked as if she was trying to say something completely different, and desperately wanted the three of them to understand.

"Don't worry, Ms. S.," Karnowski said reassuringly. "We will have you back to being boss in no time!"

Withers seemed excited by the prospect. "We're all in this together. This is the way Terrifitemps is supposed to work."

Lenore flipped through the back of the paperback one more time. "Let's see. Here it is. Spells, corn dog." She looked up at the rest of us. "This book is very thorough."

They went about assembling the ingredients one more time, slightly different and slightly more complex than the first spell (this time around, they didn't need any staples). But, with Withers's help, it went even more quickly. This time around, the spell concluded with Lenny dripping three drops of the new potion on the top of their leader's head.

"Giant economy—what was I saying?" Ms. Siggenbottom blinked. Karnowski grabbed her elbow as she wobbled unsteadily.

Their leader shook off the ghost finder's help.

"That's not necessary. I'll be fine." She looked at the crowd around her. "I'm happy to see that Terrifitemps can still be a crack team in my absence." She nodded to Lenny. "And you've gotten yourself right in the middle of it. Good job, everyone!"

She surveyed the room again. "I will need to return to my office. And Withers, you will need to find some clothes." She walked, unaided, to the door that led to the hall. "I think all of you deserve the rest of the day off. You may brief me tomorrow on anything that occurred while I was indisposed."

She shook her head. "And I never want to eat another corn dog as long as I live."

Two elevator doors opened. By some sort of silent agreement, their leader took one while the rest of the team walked into the other.

"Karnowski needs sleep!" the ghost finder announced.

"And I need clothes," Withers added.

"I think we all could use some rest," Lenore agreed. "We still have a lot to talk about. Let's reconvene in the main office at nine tomorrow and compare notes."

The elevator deposited them in the lobby on the main floor. The others waved good-bye and went their separate ways.

That was it? Lenny had hoped they could talk a bit about things now. He wouldn't have minded talking to Lenore about just about anything.

Still, just standing here, he could feel a wave of exhaustion roll over him. He could probably talk, and think, far better after a little sleep. He left the building and headed for the subway.

He was so tired his feet tended to wander a bit. He did his best to stay focused on the entry that led to the trains, swerving away from an alleyway lost in shadows. Did he glimpse a man in a raincoat there? Somewhere in the crowd, a cell phone came to life:

"You're my baby! You're my baby!"

The song sounded somehow familiar. He closed his eyes for a second in the bright sunlight. The inside of his eyelids looked bright blue.

Blue? He was forgetting something blue.

Lenny decided he didn't know what he was forgetting. He barely knew what he was thinking. He redoubled his efforts to make it down to the subway and then home.

Terrifitemps certainly was a fascinating place. He hoped, after a little rest, he could remember just how fascinating these last two dozen hours had been. And he just couldn't stop thinking about Lenore.

One thing was for certain. He finally felt like his life was going somewhere. He would go home, relax, and do something relaxing, like work on his stamp collection.

Wait a minute. He knew with a sudden certainty that something in his stamp collection was very important. Lenny realized he was holding his breath, as if he was waiting for something terrible to happen. Something terrible? From his stamps?

Lenny took a deep breath. He was going to relax and forget about everything, at least for tonight. He'd take some time tomorrow to figure out where his life was going, with or without Terrifitemps.

Lenny walked swiftly down into the subway station, ignoring the shadows that followed him down the stairs.

To be continued in:

Temporary Hauntings

Book Two of the Temporary Magic Series

About the Author

Craig Shaw Gardner is the author of more than thirty novels and fifty-odd short stories (some of them very odd.) His novelization of *Batman* was a *New York Times* bestseller, and he's a past president of the Horror Writers Association. He's written reviews and articles for numerous periodicals, ranging from *The Washington Post* to *Rampage Wrestling*, and (far more importantly) he serves as the perennial co-host (with Eric Van) of the "Kirk Polland Memorial Bad Prose Competition" every July at Readercon. He lives just north of the Center of the Universe (a.k.a. Cambridge, MA) with his wife and their two cats, George and Gracie. You can visit him online at www.craigshawgardner.com.

Other Books by Craig Shaw Gardner:
The Ebenezum Books
A Malady of Magicks
A Multitude of Monsters
A Night in the Netherhells
A Difficulty with Dwarves
An Excess of Enchantments
A Disagreement with Death

The Cineverse Cycle
Slaves of the Volcano
God Bride of the Slime Monster
Revenge of the Fluffy Bunnies

The Further Arabian Nights
The Other Sinbad
A Bad Day for Ali Baba
Scheherazade's Night Out (The Last Arabian Night)

The Dragon Circle
Dragon Sleeping (aka *Raven Walking*)
Dragon Waking
Dragon Burning

The Changeling War (as by Peter Garrison)
The Changeling War
The Sorcerer's Gun
The Magic Dead

Temporary Magic
Temporary Monsters
Temporary Hauntings
Temporary Humans

Collections
A Purple Book of Peculiar Stories
A Cold Wind in July

Other Books
The Lost Boys
Wishbringer
Batman
Back to the Future Part II
Back to the Future Part III
The Batman Murders
Batman Returns
The 7th Guest (with Matthew J. Costello)
Spider-Man: Wanted Dead or Alive
Leprechauns
Buffy the Vampire Slayer: Return to Chaos
Angel: Dark Mirror
Dark Whispers (as by Chris Blaine)
Battlestar Galactica: The Cylon's Secret

Curious about other Crossroad Press books?
Stop by our site:
http://store.crossroadpress.com
We offer quality writing
in digital, audio, and print formats.

Enter the code FIRSTBOOK
to get 20% off your first order from our store!
Stop by today!

Made in the USA
Columbia, SC
08 January 2025